Golden Angel

Clifton LaBree

© 2015 by Author, Clifton LaBree

Published by
Fading Shadows Imprint
New Boston, New Hampshire, USA

ISBN-10:1-943329-21-4
ISBN-13: 978-1-943329-21-2

Cover Design by Vivian LaBree
Also, a special thanks to Currier Flying Service, Greenville, Maine, for the photo of the deHavilland Beaver plane on the front cover.

Dedicated to my wife Pauline, and my family, with thanks for all their support and encouragement

Chapter One

Summer 1955

Retired Chief Petty Officer Alvin Starr of the U.S. Coast Guard drove his new 1955 Studebaker pickup truck along the last few miles of U.S. Route 10 where it terminated in Jacksonville, Florida at Route 95. The new route followed along the eastern coastline to northern Maine. The smooth running V/8 engine in the truck was economical and powerful. He had ordered it specially built with an overdrive transmission to improve gasoline mileage and to achieve higher speeds on the highway.

He had served twenty years in the Coast Guard in both the Atlantic and Pacific Oceans. The wound that led to his being discharged from the service was received in the Korean War. It took place while he commanded a well-armed patrol boat with orders to secure a small island off the west coast of Inchon prior to the planned amphibious landings. He and six of his men were ordered to establish navigational equipment on the island assumed to be vacant. He ran into a small arms fire-fight with twelve enemy soldiers and was wounded in the final exchange of fire when a North Korean soldier, hidden in a gun redoubt, threw a grenade in their midst.

The wound took him out of the active combat area back to the states where he recuperated with a stainless steel rod in a portion of his left leg. He was able to function as usual in most of his jobs, but his superior officer was reluctant to place him in harm's way again. He was discharged with a twenty percent disability compensation. The discharge was made at San Diego Coast Guard Headquarters where he had been stationed for the past three years.

1

Now he was heading home. Thoughts of Maine and the small town of Monson where he grew to manhood warmed his heart. He had traveled all over the world with the Coast Guard, visiting more ports than he could recall. None of them came close to capturing his affection like Maine. He stopped at a diner in Jacksonville for a cup of coffee and a hamburger. Then he filled his tank on the truck before getting on the highway. He computed that he was getting close to twenty miles per gallon with his truck, thanks to the overdrive transmission.

Alvin had traveled the same routes several times over the years, sometimes by bus or train. This trip with his new truck was a new experience. He had stopped for the night at truck stops that were open twenty-four hours. That way he could sleep safely in the bed of his truck on an air mattress and save on hotel fares. So far he had stopped four times at Tucson, San Antonio, New Orleans, and Tallahassee. The next evening he decided to stop at Richmond, Virginia, and rent a room for the night. He needed a shower really badly. Generally he drove about twelve hours every day before parking for the night.

He was optimistic about arriving the next day in Maine after Richmond. Home was not what it had once been. He knew that, but he had to touch base with that part of his life before he made any plans for the future. He would have to work. His pension and retirement would not support him full time. He was forty years old and still in good health, too young to retire to a rocking chair. The wound in his leg ached at times, but it did not keep him from doing what he wanted to do.

Near dusk he was pulling into a Howard Johnson Hotel and restaurant in the outskirts of Richmond. Over the years he had stopped there often. He parked the truck and went to the reception desk to get a room on the ground floor with easy access from the parking area. He moved his truck to a parking space in front of the room and picked up his duffel bag and shaving kit before checking out the room.

He returned to the truck to organize the bed when a light green 1952 Studebaker Champion sedan pulled into the space beside him. He noticed the Maine plates on the vehicle. A woman dressed in a blue blazer and a pair of slacks left two small children in the car while she went to the registration desk. He noted the children were a boy and a girl about seven or eight years old. He picked up a couple of K-rations and carried them into the room leaving the door open. A few minutes later, he returned to the truck to get his favorite pillow just as the woman returned to the car. He overheard parts of her conversation with the children.

"We can't stay here...they're full..."

Suddenly the two children were out of the Studebaker, screaming loudly, "Grandmother, what's wrong?"

Alvin turned to see what was happening. He saw the woman's figure drop out of sight beside the car, and he too ran to help the lady. Tears filled her haunting eyes as she desperately tried to hang onto the car door handle. He got to her before she fell to the pavement. He screamed to the children. "Kids, open the door to my room. Your grandmother is about to pass out."

The little boy rushed to hold the door open for him to carry his grandmother into the room, laying her on the closest bed. Alvin recalled that he had one man in his division that used to have similar attacks with heavy breathing, nervous tension, and losing consciousness. He checked for a pulse. It was racing dangerously high. "Children, is your grandmother a diabetic? Does she have to take insulin shots?"

The two children were hysterical with fear. "She gave herself a shot this morning at the North Carolina Army base," the boy told him with quivering lips.

"Now, you two must be calm. Help me help your grandmother. Take this money and go to the restaurant just down the walkway a few feet," he exclaimed distinctly and calmly. "Ask a waiter for a glass of orange juice and a couple of cans of cold pineapple juice. Do you understand? Tell the waiter it's an emergency. Can you do that?"

"I can do it, sir," the boy replied, taking the five dollar bill from Alvin. "Will it help my grandmother?"

"I think so. What's your name?"

"Jodi," he replied quickly. "My sister is called Melody."

"You two should not worry. She'll be fine. You can call me Mr. Al. Now hurry!"

Their grandmother placed an arm over her eyes. Tears slowly ran into her ears. Alvin got a towel from the bathroom and wiped them away. "Lady, can you hear me? Your grandchildren have gone to the restaurant to get something for you. Can you hear me?"

"Yes, I hear you...Who are you? What am I doing here in this bed? The hotel had no vacancies...," she stammered as if in a trance.

"I was in the vehicle beside your automobile and heard you say there was no room," he explained carefully. "Are you experiencing an insulin attack? I only want to help you, Ma'am."

She moved her head as if to acknowledge his question. "Yes, I waited until we stopped for the night..."

"I have some crackers and peanut butter from an Army ration pack. If I prop your head up, can you eat something?"

"Yes, thank you... I don't mean to be a bother to strangers."

"You are not a bother, lady," he calmly told her, placing a couple of pillows at her back. "Here, chew on these crackers, Ma'am. The children should be back soon with some juice for you."

She chewed one cracker and swallowed it. He placed another in her hand and wiped her brow of sweat with a towel from the bathroom. The two children ran into the room with a glass of orange juice and two small cans of Dole pineapple juice. They were frightened for their grandmother.

"Thanks, children. You did great. Your grandmother will be fine in a few minutes. Now, have her drink the orange juice you got for her. She really needs something like that now."

She smiled at Melody who leaned over the bed and offered her the glass of orange juice. She slowly drank all of the juice.

"Do not be afraid, Melody. I did not want you to see me like this," she cried softly, embracing the upset little girl.

Alvin quietly stood by and watched a transformation take place before his eyes. The grandmother quickly reacted to the crackers and cheese and the juice. Her color was better, and her eyes took on a softer look. Within a few minutes she seemed to be alert and calm. Alvin took advantage of her recovery to remove his duffel bag from the room and placed it in his truck. He called for Melody and Jodi to join him outside so that their grandmother could rest quietly.

"Your grandmother needs to rest for a while. I'll help you carry your suitcases into the room. You need it more than I do. I can sleep in the bed of my truck."

That statement seemed to please the twins who looked tired and were still concerned for their grandmother. He gave the key to the Studebaker Champion to Jodi. "Here, young man. Give these keys and purse to your grandmother in the room or place them on the table beside her bed."

Jodi did as he was requested. "We're staying in this room for the night, Grandmother. Mister Al said we could have it."

She placed an arm around Jodi and warmly embraced him. The juice and crackers were working their magic! "I'm sorry I delayed my insulin shot until you two had to see me like this. I did not want to frighten you. I'll be fine, you'll see."

Alvin returned to the room to hear what she said to Jodi. "I'm glad to see you responding so well, Ma'am. I had a man in my company who had diabetes, and I recalled how he always had crackers in his pockets for those times when he had overshot his insulin schedule. I knew that the children were scared. I'm pleased to be of assistance."

"You've been very kind, but we cannot accept your offer of the room...," she spoke in a low voice.

Alvin interrupted her. "Lady, I only took the room so that I could take a shower. As far as my sleeping in the truck, I've been doing that ever since I left San Diego, California. Compared to a lot of beds I've slept in over the past few years, my inflated mattress is like sleeping in the lap of luxury. I insist that you and the twins take the room. I'll take a shower this evening, and you can enjoy the privacy for the rest of the night and in the morning."

"Thank you for your generosity," she replied, noting the blue pants and the chevron stripes on his blue shirt. "Are you a sailor?"

"No, Ma'am. I'm a Coast Guardsman. I've just been mustered out of the service after serving for twenty years. I'm on my way back home to a little town called Monson, Maine. It's just south of Moosehead Lake. I saw your Maine plates when you drove into the parking lot. Maine folks have a tradition of looking out for each other. Where are you from?"

5

"I live in Orono, north of Bangor on the Brewer River," she replied.

"Wow, we're practically neighbors."

She chuckled at his enthusiasm. "That tradition is strong in Maine. I work at the University of Maine as a Librarian."

"I see that you also drive a Studebaker. My pickup truck is brand new. I bought it in San Diego. This is my first trip in it. I treated myself to a new truck, hoping to get in some quiet hunting and fishing once I get settled home. Incidentally, I can see that the food and drink have helped you. I hope you don't think it's bold of me, but I'd be honored to share supper with you and the twins in the restaurant just around the corner. They have a pretty good assortment on their buffet line. I've eaten here several times over the years."

"I should eat something," she replied, looking at the twins. "What do you two think? Are you as hungry as I am?"

They both replied, "Yes, Grandmother." He saw relief in their eyes that she was better.

Alvin grinned. "When I was their age I was always hungry. I'll leave so that you can get settled, and I'll meet you at the restaurant when you're ready." He picked up his shaving kit on his way out.

Twenty minutes later, they were working their way through the extensive buffet line. Alvin selected macaroni and cheese, string beans and pineapple slices. He smiled that the twins and their grandmother selected the same thing. He had an opportunity to observe the grandmother as she pondered selections.

Merci Lane was short and of medium build with high cheek bones and dark eyes that at times gave her a severe look until she smiled. Then, the lines around her eyes and mouth softened and her compassionate demeanor shined through the veneer of indifference. She had brown hair that fell about her shoulders. Her eyes were the most compelling feature on her face. They were alert and constantly surveying the world around her. Her nose was average with a slight tilt upward. He expected that she was an independent lady, and a stranger would probably call her a little distant, a person who stood her ground proudly regardless of what the world thought of her. He saw that she was in the habit of speaking her mind, a

6

reflection of the independence that partially defined her. He mused that she could be several individuals at the same time.

The twins ate ravenously. Alvin enjoyed watching them. Even though his time with the trio was short, Alvin sensed an air of sadness and anxiety present. He finished his meal and drank another cup of coffee.

"I've introduced myself to Melody and Jodi. For your information, I'm Alvin Starr. May I call you someone beside Ma'am or Grandmother?" he asked.

"Of course," she replied over a cup of tea. "My name is Merci Lane. We've just come from Fort Bragg, the large Army base in North Carolina. My son was killed in Korea two years ago. His wife and the twins have lived on base since that time. They are going to live with me for the summer and then maybe permanently," she continued, avoiding his penetrating eyes. "It has been a very stressful time for all of us. My son would want them to be with me. Their mother has a drinking problem that puts them at risk. When I arrived for a short visit, they begged to come home to Maine with me."

He saw the uncertainty and anxiety in her eyes. He looked at the children. They were alert, yet slightly withdrawn to a world of their own, and completely devoted to their grandmother. "I appreciate your sharing that with me, Mrs. Lane. They're beautiful children and are lucky to have a grandmother with the courage to act in their behalf. I also served in the Korean War. The leg wound I received there was the main reason behind my retirement from the Coast Guard. I also lost my son, Joe, in Korea. He was a soldier… My return to Maine is filled with memories and images that are just as strong and vivid as when he was a little boy like Jodi here."

She felt the depth of his pain and said, "At least you have a wife to return to," she assumed after seeing his eyes become watery. They shared a common loss that few could ever understand unless they, too, shared such a tragedy.

He avoided her inquiring look and replied in a sober voice, "Joe's mother left me for another man while I was in North Africa during World War II. Joe was in high school then. I wear the ring in remembrance because she died from leukemia two years later. My parents thought it was God's punishment for her betrayal… I reserved my condemnation. I apologize, I did not mean to get into private matters."

"Do not apologize, Chief Starr. Your loyalty to a memory is a rare gift. Every family has some burden to bear. I want to thank you for being so caring and generous. You've made this a very pleasant evening. Now that the twins are with me, I've got to take better care of myself. I'm sorry that I frightened Jodi and Melody. I promise to do better and to be faithful to my medication. Having you two in my life will be like having my son with me. What a wonderful blessing you are."

The twins responded to her remarks with smiles. They already knew how lucky they were. Alvin admired their love for her. "Jodi and Melody are truly blessed to have a grandmother who has shown courage to act when action was needed."

"You are very kind, Chief Starr."

Chapter Two

That evening Merci insisted on paying for the meals at the restaurant. Alvin conceded, telling her that he would like to take his shower right after the meal. That way he would not interfere with their routines in the morning. He could shave in the restroom of the restaurant when he went for his breakfast. There was still reluctance on Merci's part not to put him out of his room. Again, he told them that sleeping in the truck was a new adventure he enjoyed. It was getting late, and everyone was weary.

Alvin completed his shower in a very short time. "Chief Starr, you don't waste time in the shower do you?" Merci smiled.

"Old habits die hard, Ma'am. On board ships, with large crews and a scarcity of water, you're expected to rinse, lather, and rinse again so that a buddy in line can take his turn. We call them Coast Guard showers. I'm ready to turn in now. I won't disturb you in the morning. Rest well, children, and you, too, Grandmother."

"Thank you again for your generosity. We'll enjoy a night's rest. Goodnight, Chief."

"You're very welcome," he said and left the room.

Alvin was by nature an early riser. He enjoyed the calm and quiet that the dawn of a new day provided. It was an important time in his life when he not only planned the day ahead, but reviewed what had been significant and important in the events of the past day. He was leaving the Coast Guard with some reluctance and sadness. The future would probably never test him as the small maritime service had done during his twenty years of service.

His responsibilities as a chief in the Coast Guard were far greater than those of an enlisted man in the other services. He

9

commanded a patrol boat for years in all kinds of weather and with every conceivable type of mission assigned to the smallest military service in the country. Early in his career, he developed a habit of questioning the decisions he made and how they affected the men in his company. He treated them with respect and always had their interests at heart. Most of the missions involved life-threatening situations that required quick thinking and immediate action. His crews had functioned with precision and daring that saved countless lives on the dark waters of the North Atlantic and the blue waters of the Pacific.

He never failed to reward and praise exceptional performance. At the same time, he was quick to point out errors or mistakes and to suggest ways of correcting them, especially when they affected the performance of their mission. He and his crews were competent in constructing and maintaining navigation aids. Failure of any component could be disastrous, and they took that responsibility very seriously.

He remembered one incident he and his crew would never forget. He was in command of a new eighty-three-foot patrol boat in the North Atlantic, south of the Grand Banks, December of 1946. He had been conducting fisheries studies with the Canadian Coast Guard and, at the same time, double-checking all of the navigational systems in the area. Late afternoon, they received an urgent S.O.S. that always has special meaning to mariners. He locked his homing instrument on the signal and turned the boat towards its source. His heart was pounding rapidly. He had his radio man make contact with Canadian Coast Guard and with his home base at Portland, Maine. They were unable to make contact with the source of the signal. That was not unusual in itself, but it limited them not knowing what to expect. Their transponder continued to send out strong signals.

"How far out are they, Hank?" Alvin had asked his radio man.

"About ten miles on our current course. Visibility is getting poorer by the minute, and winds are increasing. We're due for a severe northeaster, Chief. I'll keep trying to make contact. Portland is sending the cutter *ACUSHNET* to aide us with helicopter on board. Estimated time of arrival is six to seven hours."

"Too late for our needs. Are there any ships close to the source?"

"None, Chief. Canadian CG will have to refuel before responding. We'll be the first and only responder for the next several hours. Our fuel is sixty percent, Chief."

"Thanks, Hank. I'm concerned with the heavy seas we're experiencing. These patrol boats are not very maneuverable in close quarters."

The sleek wooden patrol boat was travelling with all the speed their two Gray marine six cylinder engines were capable of producing. Essentially they were industrial-grade Chrysler engines. They performed well and gave very little trouble. He had the crew double-check the powerful search lights they carried fore and aft and on top of the cabin. All of the life jackets aboard had been moved to the main deck for quick use as needed. Life lines were increased, and the inflatable rafts were positioned for immediate use.

The moment they made contact, it was Alvin's responsibility to evaluate the situation, determine a course of action, and to execute that action as rapidly as possible. The North Atlantic had a fierce reputation of turning mishaps into disasters with horrendous consequences. Every one of his crew had experienced such occurrences. The Coast Guard was proud of their honorable life-saving reputation. It was the main reason that they existed.

"Chief, the source of the signal is due north."

All eyes focused ahead, trying to see through the fog and mist. A slight reflection on the surrounding clouds could be distinguished a couple of miles away. It looked as if it might be a fire! They fired several starburst flares into the air to let them know that assistance was coming to them. Slowly the flicker on the horizon grew larger and larger. It was a fire. The patrol boat did not have fire suppression capabilities, and that made the situation even more desperate.

Alvin went to the small catwalk that projected out over the nose of the boat with a megaphone. He ordered every light on the boat to be turned on. He wanted the people to know that help was imminent. He scanned the fiery scene. It was a large luxury yacht. The fire was heavily involved in the engine room and at the rear deck. Several people could be seen crowded on the elevated forward deck. They also had a narrow catwalk which was packed with frightened adults and some children. There were a few swimmers in the water. They had to be retrieved quickly, or they would not survive the freezing temperatures. Traditionally, humans did not survive but a few minutes!

Alvin knew that they had to act quickly and to get as close to the crippled craft as possible. He ordered three of the crewman to lower the rafts and to pick the people out of the water. They had priority. The high seas made it dangerous to get too close to the superstructure of the yacht. It was already tilting to the starboard away from the patrol boat. He ordered Hank to notify U.S. and Canadian Coast Guard of the urgent situation. The rafts had reached the people already in the water when a loud explosion partially lifted the yacht out of the water and almost upset the rafts filled with frightened people. Several people, including women and children on the catwalk, were thrown into the water without preservers.

Two lines with scaling hooks were thrown at the yacht to anchor the patrol boat to the superstructure. All hands pulled the craft against the burning hulk. "You people on the catwalk," Alvin hollered to be heard, "make your way down the hull toward us, women and children first. Do not jump into the water unless you have a lifejacket." There was a drop of about four feet to the deck of the patrol boat. Several women and three small children were crying as eager hands reached to pull them into the boat. One little boy about four years old had been thrown by a woman towards Alvin who caught him, but lost his grip when the boat shifted in the high seas. The boy desperately grabbed for Alvin's lifejacket harness and held on, screaming at the top of his lungs.

"You did well, son." Alvin said, hanging onto him as he turned to pass him to a Coast Guardsman.

"Where's my mother?" the boy screamed.

"We'll get her, son."

For a frantic twenty minutes they pulled survivors out of the frigid waters and deposited them onto the crowded deck of the patrol boat. They grasped any part of the survivors they could get a hold on. Some were lifted from the water by their hair and did not complain. The patrol boat was taking a beating as it was continuously being pounded against the yacht's hull. The men in the rafts had collected all of the survivors in the water. Those who were still on the forward deck and had survived the explosion were now threatened by the leaping flames that were consuming the craft at an alarming rate. Alvin saw several people still clinging to the wreckage on the yacht's catwalk.

He grabbed one of the lines and pulled himself onto the yacht. Several people were too frightened to move. "Folks, we're running out of time. Jump into the water where my crew will immediately pull you aboard the rafts. Do you understand?"

He got no response, so he physically pulled the closest man's hands from the rail and dumped him overboard, and continued until the catwalk was cleared. He had handed down four children into the strong hands of his crewmen in the rafts below. He climbed to the highest point on the twisted catwalk for a look around. The ship was slowly dipping into the Atlantic. Only a small portion of the superstructure was out of the water.

"Is anyone still on the burning yacht? Scream if you can hear me."

On the starboard side of the yacht opposite from the patrol boat, he heard the shrill hysterical voice of a child crying for its mother. Alvin was given the most devastating experience of his life as he made his way through twisted, jagged pieces of steel, ripping a large tear on his left arm and chest. It was getting dark, and he was having trouble distinguishing images in the jumbled mass of wreckage. Suddenly, in the shadows of the superstructure rigging he saw a little girl five or six years old unable to move.

"Hang on, little girl, I'm coming," he cried as loud as he could to be heard above the howling winds. He was in about four feet of water climbing over ragged debris. Just as he was within reach of her outstretched little hands, the yacht began to sink. He was standing on the roof of the wheel house when the movement threw him into deeper water. He had briefly touched the little fingers but was unable to pull her free of the entangling wreckage. He helplessly watched the child sink beneath the water. The last words she uttered were, "Mother...Mother..."

The image of that scene had been burned on his consciousness. Every small child he encountered after the

13

incident brought back the terror he experienced. It shattered his soul, and he blamed himself. He should have gotten to her sooner…. The burning hulk sank beneath the water, burying its tragedies and secrets from mortal man. The North Atlantic had claimed its victims that day, adding another tragedy to its legacy of death.

Alvin had a difficult time getting himself free of the tangled mass of steel and wood. One of the crew member helped him into the raft. "You did all you could do, Chief. Come, we've still got work to do."

Once everyone was on board, he ordered the patrol boat to make a final circle around the debris field to check for survivors. They pulled two dead bodies from the water. "Hank," Alvin cried to his radioman. "Put out a call to anyone for assistance. We're dangerously overloaded in these high seas."

They took a headcount and came up with thirty survivors on board. An hour later, a Canadian Coast Guard corvette was seen running at full speed in their direction. They quickly relieved the patrol boat of their passengers. A young Canadian ensign asked for permission to come aboard to shake Alvin's hand.

"Chief, you and your small crew have worked a miracle that will become a part of the legendary mystic of the North Atlantic. Well done, Chief Starr. We'll head back to Halifax with our passengers. Can we be of any more assistance to you?"

Still in a state of shock, Alvin looked out at the dark waters, and tears filled his eyes. He embraced the young ensign and cried like a baby: "I lost one, Ensign…a little girl and I lost her…"

* * *

"Chief Starr…Chief Starr," a soft voice woke him from the reverie.

He opened his eyes and saw little Melody looking at him through the window of the pickup cap. Her little voice and her presence at that time when he was reliving painful past events gave him a shock that Melody saw in the reflection of his eyes. He quickly climbed out of the truck and sat her on the tailgate beside him. "Little girl, you interrupted old dreams that I have lived with for a long time. Do not be afraid. You just startled me, that's all. How did you sleep last night?"

"The bed was comfortable, Mr. Al. I was the first up to take a shower. Grandmother and Jodi are getting ready. I was curious to see how you slept," she said, looking at his mattress and the hanging lantern on the ceiling.

"Climb up on the mattress, and you'll see for yourself that it's softer than a regular bed."

Melody kneeled down and stretched out on the mattress, smiling. She saw a picture of a soldier taped on the ceiling of the cap. "My father was a soldier like that," she said and crawled out onto the tailgate.

"Your father was a brave man. That picture is of my son who, like your father, died so that you and I can be free to live our lives without fear."

"My mother told us about things like that, and so did Grandmother. Why can't he come to say good-bye to Jodi and me?" she asked innocently.

That simple question was difficult for Alvin to answer. "Every person has a physical body like us who can feel pain and sorrow and joy. All of us can laugh, run and play. These are part of our physical presence. We also have a spiritual physique that is unique to each person. We all have different likes and dislikes and different ways of reacting to situations that are a part of life. When something happens to our body, the spirit is released. It's invisible so that no one can see it. I'm sure that the spirit of your father is here with you right now, Melody. You can't see him, but he's there like a protective angel looking after you."

She absorbed his words and stared at him for a few seconds. "Sometimes when I'm sad, I think of my father who used to read stories to us and rock us to sleep. I can feel that he's near me, and that makes me happy and sad at the same time."

He placed an arm around her. "I'm sure that your father is always with you, Melody. When you're sad, he's sad too. I often have the same kind of feelings for my son. Well, look who just stepped out of the room," he exclaimed.

Merci and Jodi were carrying their suitcases out to the Studebaker. "We had a very restful night, Chief. I see that our little early-bird girl found you."

"Melody and I had a wonderful visit this morning," he said. "I've shaved already and waited to see if we might have breakfast together."

15

"That would be fine," Merci agreed. "However, I insist on picking up the tab. You've been generous enough. After that, we'll hit the road again. What a difference a night's sleep makes."

Alvin lifted Melody down off the tailgate and locked it. They took the same seats in the restaurant as they had the night before. They went through the buffet line. Alvin and Merci had scrambled eggs, bacon and toast. The twins each had cereal and toast. Merci matched him with coffee cup after cup. There was an air of independence about Merci with a hint of melancholy that defied definition. It was almost as if the tragedy of her dead son still held her in bondage.

While he and Merci were enjoying their last cup of coffee, he looked around the table and said, "We're both traveling to Maine. Why don't we run in tandem? The area around Washington can be confusing. I've been through it numerous times. What do you say, Mrs. Lane?"

"That sounds fine to me. I'm not used to this heavy traffic," she replied.

"I'll lead the way then. How about setting a speed of about fifty miles per hour. Your Champion can travel faster than my truck. We should pick a speed each of us is comfortable with."

"That sounds reasonable, Chief. I'll follow you."

He looked at the twins and then at Merci with a questioning look on his face. "I was just thinking, have you or the twins ever visited the DC area?"

"No," she replied. "I was scheduled to go as a chaperone for the Corinna high school senior class, but I was ill at the time and did not make it. When they returned, the students were enthusiastic about the sites they had visited."

"I have a suggestion. I've seen most of the sites, but there is one that stands out as being a powerful emotional experience, the Tomb of the Unknown Soldier. If you want, I can lead us to Arlington Cemetery very easily. I'd be glad to do it. Even the twins will be impressed by the solemnity and peace that is present at the Tomb. It will take about an hour altogether. The decision is yours."

She looked at the twins. "I like your suggestion, Chief. It would be a worthwhile detour. I've read much about the Tomb and how the body was selected in France after World War One."

16

"I was assigned to Arlington Cemetery for a year doing ceremonial duty. The Third Army Regiment that is responsible for the sentry detail at the Tomb are the very best. It's the most sacred location in Washington, and I think the twins will remember the visit for a long time."

Chapter Three

The trip from Richmond to Washington took about three hours. They drove non-stop to Washington where Alvin led the way off Route 95 onto a street that ran beside the Potomac River to Arlington Cemetery. He pulled into a parking area on Memorial Avenue west of the Amphitheater and the Tomb of the Unknown Soldier, locking the truck and joining Merci and the twins.

"We can reach the Tomb by going through the Amphitheater to the steps that overlook the Tomb," he told them and turned to Merci, "You did very well keeping pace, Mrs. Lane."

"Thank you. You set a reasonable speed, Chief. This place has the same feel as a church," she said in a pensive voice, looking out across the fields of crosses and Stars of David all in perfect alignment. "They represent the price we have paid for freedom."

Alvin nodded in agreement and led them to the Tomb. The twins were also mesmerized by the multitude of crosses as far as the eye could see. The cemetery was not as filled with visitors as it was on weekends. They paused at the top of the stairs of the Amphitheater, looking down at the Tomb. There they watched the sentinel in a perfect dress uniform with white gloves, holding a polished rifle with attached bayonet. The sentinel takes twenty-one steps across the mat in front of the Tomb, turns, and faces the Tomb for twenty-one seconds. Then the sentinel repeats the walk. This is representative of the highest military tribute, the twenty-one-gun salute. The soldier was stoic and seemingly oblivious to the people who may be watching him.

They walked closer to the Tomb. Alvin explained to them how the soldier spent hours preparing for the honor of being a sentinel. Many volunteered for the position, but few were chosen. The sentinels are part of the U.S. Army's Third Infantry Regiment stationed at Fort Meyers at the Arlington Cemetery. The sentinels are rotated on one or two hour tours of duty depending on the weather. Night and day, rain or shine, the sentinels walk their honored post to protect the Unknown.

A squad of soldiers appeared, coming around the Amphitheater for the change of guard routine. They marched in perfect cadence with a sergeant in command, stopping at the Tomb. Alvin told Merci and the twins that the ritual they were about to witness was carried out with every change of guard. The sergeant inspected the rifle of the man currently on duty and that of the replacement sentinel. White gloves worn by all of the soldiers are soaked in water so that they may better grasp the rifle. Every move is orchestrated to pay tribute to the Unknown. The squad marched away to Fort Meyers.

Merci could not control the tears that filled her eyes. It was an emotional experience. Alvin had to fight to control the struggle for release. The Tomb evokes deep emotions in most people. A simple reading of the inscription etched in the marble stone of the Tomb touches the heart strings: HERE LIES IN HONORED GLORY AN AMERICASN SOLDIER KNOWN BUT TO GOD.

The twins observed the scene with pensive grace, feeling the sensation of peace that permeates the area. It is a place that many people find difficult to leave. Alvin watched Merci closely in case she was overcome with emotion, but she held up well. They walked slowly in silence back to the vehicles. Small talk or chatter was out of place in the cemetery.

"When would you like to stop for lunch, Mrs. Lane? There are several places along the highway."

"The twins are getting ready to eat something," she told him. "Thank you for bringing us to this beautiful place. You're correct; it evokes powerful emotions. It makes me proud to be an American."

He nodded his head in agreement. "You're not alone, Mrs. Lane. I'll get us out of Arlington back on the highway and stop at the next place that looks appropriate. I'll need gasoline soon. A short rest stop is in order. Anytime you want to stop, just put your signal light on, and we'll pullover." He held the door open

19

for her to get into the Studebaker. "By the way, how much longer can you drive before you need to stop for the night?"

"I can go for another six or seven hours. We're anxious to get home, but getting overtired can be dangerous."

"We can make it across the George Washington Bridge in about four or five hours. I've had better luck staying in Connecticut than in New York. Stamford has a nice motel that is reasonably priced and clean."

"That sounds like a logical goal," she said, starting the automobile.

"OK," he said, rushing to his truck.

They left Arlington Cemetery and got back on 95. A few miles past the Potomac River, he pulled into a service area that had a Howard Johnson restaurant. Merci demanded that she pay for the lunch, and he let her. She got out of the Studebaker to look at her right front tire. It was a little low on air.

"I felt the car pull to the right," she exclaimed.

There was a Mobil service station at the far end of the rest area. "I'll drop the car off to the station for them to check the tire for leaks if you'll give me the keys. I'll meet you at the restaurant shortly."

She handed the keys to Alvin, "Thanks for being so helpful, Chief."

"Can I go with you, Mr. Al?" Jodi asked.

"Of course, Jodi," he smiled at his grandmother. "Us guys have got to stick together."

She laughed and took Melody's hand, leading her into the restaurant.

The Mobil station was not busy, so Alvin was able to drive the Studebaker onto a lift. Two attendants began to change the tire. Alvin and Jodi walked back to the restaurant to join Merci and Melody. The walk felt good to exercise the legs. An hour later, all of them returned to the Mobil station where the attendant told them the tire had a slow leak. They both filled up with gasoline.

Before they left the station, Alvin climbed into his pickup bed to get a small box. He opened it and took out a half dozen Hershey's Tropical nutrition bars. They were traditionally a part of the Army's famous D Field Ration. Packaged rations were a must for men in combat or other duty stations where

20

they could not partake of hot food. Every Coast Guard boat had large supplies of the rations. He walked to Merci's Studebaker.

"Here are some nutrition bars made by Hershey. They're not as sweet as their chocolate bars, but they're very nutritious. Each bar has 600 calories and is capable of sustaining a person for several hours. This may be a good item for you to carry with you, Mrs. Lane. I think you kids will like them, too. We'll plan to stop in a couple of hours for a comfort stop, okay?"

"You have taken us under your wing and shepherded us with good humor and generosity, Chief. Thank you. Semper Paratus seems to be a way of life with you."

"Maine people look after Maine people." He smiled and got back into his truck.

Two hours later, they stopped on the New Jersey Thruway for a restroom stop. Alvin asked the twins if they would like to ride with him for a change. They were eager to accept.

"By the way, Mrs. Lane, if you like country music there's a good station in Wheeling, West Virginia, WWVA. They send out a strong signal that even reaches into Maine and New Hampshire."

"I like all kinds of music. My favorites are balladeers like Eddy Arnold, Hank Snow, and Jim Reeves. This has been a long trip. The twins are getting a little fidgety. Your new Studebaker pickup truck stands out on the road. Thanks for giving the kids a break. Incidentally, your D-ration bars are excellent. It would be a good one for me to carry in my purse," she said, getting into her sedan.

"I thought you would do that," he said. "I'll keep the twins with me until we pass over the George Washington Bridge." He saw that she was getting more tired. "Is New Haven too much for you today? We can stop anywhere you would like. I certainly don't want to push you to your limit."

She started the car and replied, "I'll be fine. Driving into the sun was tiring. It's at our back now. New Haven sounds right. That will be our last overnight stop. I have to admit it will be a relief to arrive in Maine."

"You're a strong lady, Mrs. Lane. The twins are fortunate to have you. Promise me that you'll signal to stop if you get over tired."

"I promise, Chief."

The new truck had seat belts for three passengers. Melody sat in the middle next to Alvin, watching him shift gears with the lever on the steering wheel post. She finally asked, "Why do you do that? Grandmother doesn't move that stick like you do."

"You're right, Melody. Your grandmother's car has what they call an automatic transmission. The shifts are made without moving the lever. If you noticed, she has only a brake pedal on the floor. I have a clutch pedal and a brake pedal. The automatic makes driving easier."

For the next three hours, the twins bombarded him with questions about Maine and how was the weather different from North Carolina. They wondered how they would like going to school in a strange place and questioned him if fourth grade in Maine was the same as in North Carolina? He told them they would see little difference between the two states. He also mentioned that he had moved about frequently in the Coast Guard when his son was their age. Schools were pretty much the same all over the country.

He casually asked them how their mother felt about them going to Maine? He knew it was none of his business, and he did not want to pry, but he thought it odd that a young mother would voluntarily give up such two precious children. They were alert, curious, and seemed to be content to move in with their grandmother. They told him that their mother often had friends at the apartment that drank a lot and were loud. Sometimes they woke up in the middle of the night to shouting and angry words being exchanged. He asked if they were ever afraid?

Jodi was quick to reply. "Almost every night one soldier would get drunk and talk loud. He hit Melody once when she told him she was scared. Our mother had terrible arguments with him after that. When Grandmother came for a visit, she asked us if we wanted to come to live with her. The day we left, Mother had been drinking most of the night. She told us we were going to be better off with Grandmother until she could come to get us."

"Your mother loves you enough to know when you're better off," he said, wondering how he would feel if he was in the same situation.

"She was glad to see us leave, Jodi," Melody exclaimed in a forceful manner. She had been quiet for much of the time.

Alvin had assumed that she was the more passive of the two. While they were riding with him, he observed that Melody seemed slightly withdrawn.

Jodi quickly qualified his sister's outburst. "Sometimes when she got out of bed after being scared, Mother scolded her and told her to get back to her room while she and her friends argued and talked loud for hours at a time."

Alvin better understood the two innocent children now after listening to their expressions of uncertainty about the future. No child should be threatened or frightened in their own home. He had seen similar situations with service personnel. Long absences make for unhappiness, and lonely women surrounded by young men found it easy to stray from their vows.

A mile before the George Washington Bridge, he alerted the twins that they would soon be going over the famous bridge. If they looked closely at the Hudson River below them, they would see a lot of different boats. Melody was frightened being so high in the air on the top tier passageway. He reached over and placed an arm about her shoulders. She placed her head against him. "Don't be frightened, Melody. We'll be off the bridge shortly. Do either of you need to stop for the rest room?"

They both said, "No."

Melody held on to his arm. She felt comfortable with their new found friend. Alvin was touched by her response to him. He had read somewhere that the greatest gift a person can receive is to be loved and trusted by a small child. It brought back memories of that child with the golden curls he could not save from a horrible drowning death.

"We'll continue for a short distance in New York. Once we reach New Haven, Connecticut, we'll stop at a Howard Johnson motel and restaurant. I'm beginning to get a little hungry. I've got some of those Hershey nutrition bars in the glove compartment in front of you, Jodi. Would you get one for me? If you and Melody want one, help yourselves." He checked Merci in the rear view mirror. "Your grandmother is doing just fine. She must be getting tired; it's been a busy day."

The stay at Stamford was a welcome relief for Merci. She was more tired than she let on, yet Alvin saw the darker lines around her eyes and mouth. He had gone to register them at the reception desk while she and the twins stayed at the vehicles. He returned with the key and pointed to a room close to the entrance of the restaurant.

"I'll meet you at the restaurant," he said. "If it's okay with you, I paid for the room, and you can pay for supper. I'm ready for a good steak tonight."

"You're spoiling us, Chief. I think a steak is in order. We'll meet you in the restaurant after we move into the room."

"I'll shower right after eating so that you can settle in for the night," he replied. That evening after he had taken his shower, he collected his bag and was ready to leave the room. "Goodnight, kids and you, too, Grandmother. Tomorrow at this time, we'll be home and glad to be there."

He walked towards the door when Melody ran to him and put her arms around him. He kneeled to her. "Goodnight, Melody. I'll see you in the morning." He kissed her on the forehead as she wrapped her arms around his neck.

"Goodnight, Mr. Al." It was a show of affection that brought tears to his eyes.

Merci watched what had taken place, relieved to see that Melody had responded to his gentle ways. She had been worried about her granddaughter. "Goodnight, Chief. You've gained another friend."

"How lucky I am," he replied and walked out the door to his truck.

Chapter Four

That night, Melody's hug gave Alvin pause to reflect on where he was going and what he was going to do with his life. It was a question he had been attempting to answer even before he was informed of his retirement from the Coast Guard. It had all started one day when he was off the Virginia coast in one of the new patrol boats when an SOS call came from a stranded fishing boat that had run out of fuel about ten miles off the coast. While he was answering the emergency call, a message was received from his port commander to return to base as soon as possible. There was no explanation for the order. He furnished fuel to the pleasure fishing yacht and turned around to report as requested.

When he tied up to the Coast Guard dock at Portsmouth, Virginia, he was met by his superior officer, Captain Lynch. "Chief, have your boatswain mate secure the patrol boat. Someone wants to speak to you in my office."

"Yes, Sir," he had replied. "What's this about, Captain?"

"You'll see, Chief. Go right into my office. I'll be in a little later."

He had a bad premonition when he opened the door and was confronted by a young Army major. "I'm Chief Starr. Captain Lynch said you wanted to see me, Sir... Is this about my son, Joe?" he had blurted out, suddenly feeling weak and nauseous.

"Chief, I have the very unpleasant duty to inform you that your son, Sergeant Joseph Starr, was killed in action in Korea, two days ago."

He screamed, "No... no... I knew it was something like that. Are you sure, Major?" He fell into a seat nearby, cradling his head in his arms and wept. His main reason for living had been his only son, Joe. "Why...?" he cried, "Why...?"

25

The major placed a comforting hand on his shoulder. "Go ahead, Chief. I have no way of knowing how difficult this is for you, so I'll dispense with the platitudes. It may help you to know that I contacted his company commander and asked how Sergeant Starr died. He told me that your son had exposed himself to enemy fire when he ran to the aid of one of his squad members that had been wounded. While he was dragging the wounded man back to secure lines, he was raked by enemy machine gun fire and died instantly. The wounded man survived. I have with me the Silver Star medal and the Purple Heart medal and their accompanying citations. Your son was a very brave soldier. I'm so sorry for your loss, Chief."

Alvin was in a different world. He heard the words of the major, but they did not ease the pain. His world was torn to pieces. He could not accept the fact that Joe was not coming home. Captain Lynch quietly entered the office and surveyed the scene. He told the Army major that he could leave the medals and personal belongings on his desk.

"I pray that God will comfort you in this dark hour of loss, Chief Starr. Good-bye."

Captain Lynch bid the major good-bye. "We'll take good care of the Chief, Major. We have a tradition of looking after our own."

"I understand, Captain. I begged off on this duty, but... Thank you for your kind hospitality, Sir."

Alvin heard the two officers talking. He wanted to thank the major and to tell him he understood his position, but the words just did not come. The pain was too severe. He had seen death in combat and in accidents at sea, but this was personal, his own flesh and blood. That day, the primary motivation for his life was taken away from him. He was set loose on an ocean of uncertainty. The age old question that every man asks in time of tragedy, "Where do I go from here?" dominated his consciousness. Alternatives were plentiful but specific plans were always lacking. He was truly a ship without a rudder.

Uncertainty was compounded when he was informed that he was being forced to retire. It was a time when all of the services were facing austere economical challenges. Once he learned that his days in service were numbered, he actively began to examine the future. He could not simply retire to a rocking chair.

His first decision was to purchase the new Studebaker pickup truck. He rewarded himself for the first time in years. Then he visualized the possibility of going into business of booking ocean fishing expeditions. He was well qualified to handle that type of business, and a part of him liked the idea.

A second alternative had been in the back of his mind for several years, ever since he had served with an aviation unit in Alaska. He had talked with several aviators who had taught him how to fly a few types of aircraft the Coast Guard used daily. One of his close friends was an aviator who retired after thirty years in the service, building a private business of transporting people and supplies into the wilderness areas of Alaska.

The second alternative had a lot of appeal and presented a challenge. He liked challenges! Every pilot he talked to told him essentially the same thing. If he was going to do some bush piloting in any part of the country, the best planes to purchase and to fly were the deHavilland Beaver DHC-2 or a Cessna 180 or 185.

The closer he got to Maine, the more he thought about the second option. It could be fun and exciting, more or less a continuation of what he had been experiencing for years in the Coast Guard. He had saved enough money to purchase a used aircraft. The Folsom's Flying Service in Greenville, Maine, was a good place to start asking questions. It was one of the most active float plane centers in the country. He had half- heartedly talked with them about such an enterprise. They told him that there were many opportunities in the area to put an aircraft to work. The Maine Forest Service gives out contracts annually for flying forest fire patrols into the Allagash Region of northern Maine.

That morning, he was up earlier than usual. Still dressed in his blue pants and light blue shirt, the standard Coast Guard undress uniform, he stretched his legs, checking the tires of Merci's Studebaker and his pickup. The sun had just peaked out of the eastern horizon. A good omen for their last day on the heavily traveled eastern seaboard.

He saw Merci and the twins come out of the room with their luggage. "Well, I thought I was the only early bird around," he exclaimed. "I hope you all slept well."

"We slept the sleep of the exhausted, Chief," Merci told him, placing the luggage in her car trunk.

"Are you ready for breakfast?"

"Yes, coffee will be welcome. The twins are always ready to eat. They have healthy appetites."

Both parties were anxious to get home, so they kept their stops to a minimum. Alvin maintained a constant pace of fifty miles per hour from Stamford, Connecticut, through to the Kennebunk, Maine, rest area where they stopped for midday lunch and refueling of the vehicles. The twins rode with him since they crossed over the Mystic River in Charlestown, Massachusetts. He noticed that the steady grind was beginning to show on Merci. She was getting tired.

"Are we pushing too hard for you, Grandmother?" Alvin asked her as they were heading into the convenience center. "You look tired."

She avoided his searching eyes. "I'll be all right," she replied.

"That does not answer my question. I don't mean to pry into private affairs. I was only thinking of your welfare. We've got about three hours from Kennebunk. I feel better just crossing the state line into Maine," he grinned. "I apologize for my rudeness."

"I appreciate your concern, Chief, but when I tell you that I'll be all right, I really mean it. End of conversation."

For the final leg of their journey, the twins rode in the truck with Alvin. He told Merci that he would stop at a rest area south of the Newport exit. He mentioned to the twins that he was returning to the house and town where he was born and grew up as a little boy. His parents were living there when he joined the Coast Guard. He had been married with a little boy younger than they were. They asked him what it would be like to live in Maine with their grandmother working at the university.

"Well, kids, there will be a lot of sports you can watch and fun events like watching the Army and Air Force cadets drill on the athletic field like you must have seen in North Carolina. You should be proud of your grandmother. She has a very important job with the University of Maine. You two will have to promise me that you'll be good with her and help her when she asks for something. She's the best friend you'll ever have in this world."

"Can you be our friend?" Melody asked him.

"I already am, Melody. One never has too many friends."

He told them about living in a small town like he grew up in. His hunting and fishing trips with his father and uncles were happy times, and he shared some of them with the twins. Time passed quickly, and before he realized it, the rest area turn-out was straight ahead. He parked in the designated parking area and went around to get a small box from the back of his truck. Merci parked beside him and got out of the car.

Alvin handed a small box to each of the twins. "These are Army D-rations. I have plenty of them. These are for you two. I'll always remember this trip with you, Melody and Jodi. This is a new beginning, and I wish you all the best. Good-bye and thanks for the company on the long trip."

"Good-bye, Uncle Al." Melody held out her arms to embrace him. "Will we see you again?"

He kneeled down to hold her. "If you ever need a friend, you can call on me. I'll leave my address with your grandmother. Good-bye, little girl. You and your brother have been great troopers. This is not really good-bye; let's call it a so-long."

Jodi was sober when he embraced the kind stranger who had, over the course of two days, become a friend they looked up to. "Thank you for helping us."

"It was my pleasure, Jodi. Look after your grandmother. You'll be the little man of the house. Promise?"

"I promise."

Merci watched the way the twins had reacted to his kindness. He had held out the hand of friendship, and they basked in the security of his protection. She helped them into the Studebaker and turned to Alvin. "How does a person say thank you for such unselfishness? You've made a difficult journey into a marvelous adventure."

They quietly exchanged address cards. He spoke first. "I want you to know that this short interval with you and the twins has enriched my life more than you'll ever know. I left California filled with regrets and disappointment that my career in the Coast Guard had ended so quickly. Now, I feel energized to take on the world and to begin a whole new chapter in my life. I thank you and the twins for helping to make that happen. I wish you the very best, Merci. You have bravely taken on a new responsibility. I admire you for reaching out to Melody and Jodi. If you're ever in need of a friend, please call on me and I'll be there."

It was a sober parting, more difficult than either of them had imagined. She deftly wiped a tear from her left eye. "We've been together for such a short time, yet I feel as if we've known each other longer."

"I've had that same feeling, too."

"Good-bye, Chief. May your dreams and hopes for the future bear fruit. You deserve that. Thanks for everything and especially being so supportive with the twins. Your generosity has touched each of them, and you've won their affection even though we're really strangers. That's an accomplishment to be proud of."

"They're our hope for the future and are very precious kids, much like their unselfish grandmother."

He paused a moment and held out his arms to her. She came into them, and they embraced. He could smell the subtle aroma of wild roses in her hair. She kissed him on the cheek and turned away from their embrace.

He walked to his truck and waved. "Until next time, Merci."

She returned his wave and replied, "Until next time, Chief."

Alvin watched the green Studebaker sedan go around the corner out of sight before he started his truck. All of sudden he felt alone. Watching the twins and Merci continue on without him was a strange experience. For the past two days he had felt needed and was happy to be of assistance to good people that appreciated it. It was a letdown he did not expect.

The road from Newport to Monson was one he had traveled often during his forty years. The last time was when his father had died of a heart attack three years ago. His mother had died several years prior to his father. He was alone in the world. He had lost both parents, a wife, and a beloved son all in a span of a few years. An older sister had tragically died in a car accident in 1943. He was the lone survivor of the clan, and his return to his roots were giving him an overwhelming sense of loss. He was the only survivor of the Starr family.

That portion of north central Maine that included Monson was struggling to survive economically. Opportunities for employment were few and far between. The two slate quarries in Monson had closed. The Second World War had given a lot of the young men a chance to see the outside world and what it had to offer for a better life for themselves and their families. Many did not return. In 1955 the town was still viable, but it was holding on by a thread. Jobs were only available in Greenville and surrounding towns like Guilford and Dover-Foxcroft.

Farming was difficult in the rocky soil and the cold winter months. He had first-hand experience with that aspect of rural living. As a child, he recalled many happy times, and they never went hungry like some during the difficult depression years. They always had a cow for milk and cream, pigs for bacon and ham, and a large garden that constantly needed weeding as he recalled. They also had a large supply of apples from the half dozen trees beside the garden plot. Some of the trees produced four or five different varieties of apples. His grandfather had grafted the variety of apples onto the existing root system. Today it was a lost art. They always ate well at the Starr family, but money was scarce. It was one of the main reasons he selected the Coast Guard after he graduated from Monson Academy high school. Now the Academy was closed, and students went to Dover.

He could see the white Cape Cod style home on the western side of the main road from Guilford to Monson a long ways before he turned into the driveway. Coming home to an empty house was a painful experience. He checked the roofs on the house, shed, and barn for recent damage and found none. The neighbors had kept the open fields mowed. The old house seemed to be weathering well.

He opened the front door and turned on the lights. About twenty years before they had installed electricity and a modern bathroom. What a treat that was for the entire family, especially his mother and sister. Leaving the door open to air the interior of the house, Alvin walked directly to the kitchen where a black cook stove had provided most of the heat for the downstairs of the house. The woodbox was still half-full of wood. He grinned. It seemed empty most of the time when it was his job to keep it filled to the brim. It was a long walk from the shed and barn to the kitchen with an armful of dry hardwood.

31

Tired and melancholic, Alvin ate one of his nutritious Hershey bars and went to bed in his old room upstairs looking out over the Russell Mountains. He had the best location in the house to watch the sunset. That night it was most spectacular. By mid-summer the sun seemed to set down onto the highest peak of the Russells, as if it had been speared. The old house was filled with happy memories. They had been poor, but they worked hard and became self-sufficient. Taking care of each other was a way of life that sustained them well. Everyone in town was feeling the same pressures.

The next morning he went downtown to set up his mail and to buy a few groceries in the one small store left in town. Coming out of the store, he met an old classmate and friend, Lois Carson.

"Is that you, Alvin?" she asked.

"Hi, Lois," he replied. "I just got back in town last night."

"I hardly recognized you in your uniform. It's been a long time since we walked to school together. Gee, it's nice to see you. Are you home for good or just visiting?"

"I've retired from the Coast Guard, Lois. I'm not sure just what I'm going to do. Are there any new industries in the town?" he asked.

"There's a new furniture plant down where the old Portland Monson Slate Company used to be. Say, we've got an alumni dance coming up in a couple of weeks. I'd let you take me if you ask," she smiled.

She hadn't changed. He grinned. Lois had a tendency to say what was on her mind. Her husband, Carl Carson, was Alvin's best friend in town. They had spent a lot of time together hunting and fishing over the years. "I'd like that, Lois. I'm sorry about Carl. He was a good friend."

"It still hurts, Alvin. He was so good to me," she cried.

"A lot of good people paid the ultimate sacrifice during the war, Lois. I'm still having a hard time accepting Joe's death."

She embraced him. "Of course, your Joe... Life in this town will never be the same, Alvin. The town is slowly dying. Most of the men who went away during the war have not come back. They found better opportunities elsewhere. What are you going to do, Al?"

"I'm not sure, Lois. I plan to speak to the people in Greenville at Folsom's Airways about the potential of establishing a light plane courier service, taking hunters and fishermen into remote locations. I'm still exploring alternatives."

"Well, I've got to run. It's so nice to have you back home, Al. Will you still have the same phone number?" she asked.

"I expect so. Let's keep in touch, Lois. You're looking good. Your Finnish ancestry is serving you well."

She smiled, as she did often. "Having an old friend near is a comfort."

When he arrived in Greenville, at the southern tip of Moosehead Lake, he was surprised. It had always attracted some summer tourists, but today he found the center of the village area crowded with tourists. He went to Folsom's Airways in the little harbor at the village. They did a brisk sight-seeing business with summer tourists. Folsom's was primarily responsible for the large amount of float plane traffic off the lake.

He watched a deHavilland Beaver take off with five passengers. The throaty Pratt and Whitney Wasp engine had a distinct sound when it was under full power taking off with a loaded aircraft. He had a few years experience with the Coast Guard flying in the two-engine Grumman amphibious aircraft doing search and rescue missions. He was acutely aware of the dangers of a float plane making a turn in heavy seas or high winds. If the pilot taxied so that the wind struck the plane from the side, it could easily be tipped enough to submerse one float and possibly tip the plane over.

He had a good conversation with the owner at Folsom's who told him that the summer months were the most profitable with sight-seeing flights and forest fire patrols for the Maine Forest Service. The chances of making a living from sportsmen expeditions were doubtful at best. He also echoed what he had been told by others – the best bush plane was the Beaver, with the Cessna 180 or 185 being competent alternatives.

To Alvin's surprise, there was a Beaver being rebuilt at a Bangor airport and would be offered for sale upon proper certification. He jumped at a chance to closely look one over and to evaluate the cost versus his ability to pay for the plane. He knew that maintenance was high for all aircraft and was cautious about overextending himself.

Two days after his conversation with the owner at Folsom's, Alvin was on his way to Bangor to take a look at the Beaver. When he arrived, the aircraft was completely disassembled, and the airframe was being tested for structural damage and fatigue. The engine was stripped, undergoing a total rebuild back to original specifications. The price was within his ability to pay, and he left his name and address with the repair shop, obtaining the guarantee of a first refusal once the plane had passed all of its certification requirements. The Bangor shop planned to sell the plane with landing wheels. Alvin would have Folsom's replace them with a set of new pontoons for landing on water. It was an easy adjustment to switch the pontoons to skis for snow and ice conditions.

He felt good leaving the shop. He had made the first step in carrying out his plans for the future and was excited about the possibilities. He checked his watch. It was noon. He thought of the twins and decided to pay them a visit. It was Saturday, so they would not be in school. Just in case, he called ahead to tell them he was in the area.

Merci answered the phone. "Hello."

"Merci Lane?" he asked.

"Yes, is that you, Chief?" she asked.

"I came to Bangor to look at an airplane and thought of you and the twins."

"Your timing is perfect. I promised the twins a cookout with hot dogs and hamburgers on the charcoal grill. You're welcome to join us. The twins will be pleased to see you again. I've also invited a few friends from school."

"Thanks for the invitation. I can be there in a half hour."

The small town of Alton was on Route 95, north of Bangor. He found the house sitting on a small hillside surrounded with apple orchards in full bloom. It was a white New Englander home with a steep pitched roof to readily shed snow in the wintertime. Merci's Studebaker was parked beside a barn that had been converted into a screened patio to keep out mosquitoes. It was a pleasant setting for a home. Just as he turned off the ignition key, Jodi came running to him.

"Hi, Mister Al. Grandmother told us to expect you. I saw you coming up the driveway." He embraced Alvin and pointed to the screened walkway in the barn. "We're going to have a cookout."

"That's what your grandmother told me," Alvin replied.

"Melody is in her room changing clothes. I was playing kind of rough with her and ripped her shirt."

Alvin smiled. "Well, things happen. Here comes your grandmother."

"Hello, Chief." She greeted him with a firm handshake. "Melody will be down shortly. Come on into the barn to meet some friends of mine from the University."

They walked into the screened area of the barn set up with tables and chairs around a burning charcoal grill. "Folks, I want you to meet our friend who escorted us safely along the Atlantic seaboard." Alvin saw a couple his age rise from their chairs. "Chief Alvin Starr, this is Jim and Valerie Foster, friends of many years."

"How do you do?" Alvin held out his hand to Jim. "I'm pleased to meet you. I happened to be in Bangor and took a chance on coming."

"It's a pleasure, Chief. My wife, Valerie, is Merci's assistant. I'm a forestry instructor. Merci's barn is the envy of her friends."

"It was nice of you to help, Merci. I'm glad to meet you, Chief," Valerie shook his hand. "She was exhausted from the long drive."

"What are you planning to do now that you're retired, Chief?" asked Jim.

Before Alvin could respond, Melody ran into the barn directly into Alvin's arms. She was all smiles. "Hi, little Miss Sunshine," he exclaimed, kneeling to put her down.

"I was afraid you would not come to see us," she cried. "Would you like to see our rabbits?"

"I'd love to, Melody."

She took his hand to lead him to the rear of the barn where two white rabbits were eating lettuce in a cage. "They love lettuce. Don't they have the cutest little noses?"

"They certainly do, Melody. Is lettuce their favorite food?" he asked, pleased to see her level of enthusiasm. A band of trust had developed between them over the past two days together on the road. Her acceptance of him without reservation gave him a warm feeling.

"They love lettuce and other vegetables. Grandmother told us that the rabbits are twins, too," she replied, still holding on to his hand. "She also told Jodi and me that we could help with the hamburgers and hot dogs. Do you like hot dogs?"

"One of my favorite foods, Honey. It's a great day for a barbecue. Your grandmother's barn is really nice. You and Jodi should be happy here. I'm glad for the two of you."

"It is a neat place. We take walks in the orchard. Yesterday Jodi and I saw two deer."

They returned to the screened section of the barn where Alvin noticed another man had joined the gathering. Merci took the tall, dark man by the arm and introduced him with a big smile. "Chief, I want you to meet Merle Stanchfield. He's an English professor, and you're the first to know, we just got engaged."

Chapter Five

One year later, Summer 1956.

Alvin sat on the open deck of his log cabin overlooking Lily Bay at Moosehead Lake. He was reviewing the past year of his life in search of some direction for the future. The recent past had more changes for him than any he could recall. He was quick to realize that the family homestead did not serve his needs. It was full of vivid memories of happier days that he could carry with him wherever he went.

An old friend in town made him a generous offer for the house and sixty-five acres of land, and he took it. He had located an isolated log cabin with twenty acres of land and a generous amount of lake frontage on Lily Bay. He fell in love with the place the first visit. The cabin made it possible for him to build a dock on the lake in which he could secure the deHavilland Beaver float plane he had purchased in Bangor. While the plane was being readied for service and certification, he went to flying school at the Bangor airport to get his license to fly. He had flown a lot with the Coast Guard, so it was easy for him.

Being in Bangor he often visited Jodi and Melody at Merci's place in Alton. The twins were a source of enjoyment. Over the past year they had become like a family for him. Their affection for him was complete. Melody became more open with him than she did with Merci. Her shyness disappeared whenever he turned into the driveway. She was always happy to share those things she liked to do with her Uncle Al.

One day when he stopped to take them out to lunch, Melody had told him that she was taking violin lessons. Merci and Alvin both observed that music was an important vehicle for her to express herself. She liked all styles of music, but those

37

soft ballads, contemporary and traditional, that spoke to the heart were her favorites, and they invigorated her ability to talk more openly about what she thought of certain things and situations around her. She was exploring the depth of her senses and felt empowered by the experience. Merci had rented an instrument for her lessons from the teacher.

One Saturday when Alvin attended flight school, he stopped early at Merci's with a surprise for Melody. His mother and father had been very musical. His mother played the piano, and his father the violin. Both played at town events. Alvin was more interested in the piano, so his mother gave him regular lessons on the instrument for several of his childhood years. When he sold the house, he had the piano moved to the log cabin where he passed time playing current popular songs. His favorite was country and folk music. Irish and Scottish ballads also continued to be very special to him.

The violin his father had played was of German manufacture. His father had told him that it had a beautiful tone equal to the finest Italian instruments. Alvin never reached that level of expertise. He was determined to give it to Melody. Merci graciously greeted him as he turned into the driveway. Over the past year, they had become good friends. She smiled as he climbed out of the truck.

"I have something for the twins, Merci. I hope you approve," he said as he shook her hand.

"Whenever you pay a visit, it's the highlight of the kid's day. You're very generous," she said, watching with interest as he opened the tailgate of the truck.

"First of all, I've got a pup tent and sleeping bag for Jodi. Maybe one of his cub scout friends will sleep out with him some night." He was all smiles as he piled the tent on the front steps of the house.

"He'll love that, Chief. They've gone with Merle to get some groceries," she said.

"I also have something for Melody that belonged to my father and my grandfather." He unwrapped the case from a blanket and showed her the instrument.

"Oh, my sakes alive, it's beautiful, Chief."

He plucked the strings and tuned it. "I just stopped in town to get a new set of strings. The bow is still fine. The way Melody has warmed to music has gladdened my heart. I came from a home that was filled with music. It was a wonderful experience. I still play the piano at my cabin," he told her.

"The twins will be pleased with your generosity. The gift of music is a wonderful thing. Thank you so much. So you play the piano, too?"

"You and Merle have not made it up to Lily Bay yet. The welcome mat is always out, but I understand you have a full plate working and caring for the twins. The plane is stored at Folsom's temporarily. My flying course will soon be over and I can take the twins up for a plane ride."

"When you retired, you certainly did not intend to sit in a rocking chair, did you?" she laughed.

He smiled, "That may come eventually, but for now, things are looking good. I'm excited with the prospects of shuttle runs into the wilderness. The Maine Forest Service has given me the promise of a contract for daily patrols as soon as I'm certified."

"I'm glad for you, Chief. You deserve some happiness."

"Well, I've got a class to catch in Bangor. It was nice talking to you, Merci. Give my best to the twins and to Merle," he said, closing the tailgate on the truck.

"So long, Chief," she replied with a wave of her hand.

That night, after Alvin returned home, he received a phone call from Jodi and Melody. "We were surprised with your gifts, Uncle Al. I'm going to set up the tent beside the barn and will sleep in it tonight. It has a net to keep out the mosquitoes."

"You'll need it, Jodi. Trust me, summer nights in Maine are filled with swarms of mosquitoes and no-see-ems. In North Carolina you call them midges. I'm glad you like them. It's been almost a year that you've been in Maine. Have you heard from your mother?"

"She's called a few times and we get a letter once in a while. I think she's going to move away from the Army base. She mentioned the possibility of coming to Maine," Jodi told him.

"Well, that may work out, Jodi."

"Melody is bursting at the seams to talk with you, Uncle Al. Thank you."

"You're welcome, Jodi. Hello, Melody."

"I'm sorry we missed you, Uncle Al. I've never had such a wonderful gift. The violin is beautiful. I'm so anxious to try it out. You're very generous to us, Uncle Al. Uncle Merle thought

39

it was too expensive for a child to use. Sometimes I think he doesn't like us living with Grandmother."

"Give him some time, Melody. As we get older, changes in our lives are more and more difficult to accept." He thought that children have a gift for perceiving unspoken thoughts in people. He did not want to get involved in differences that could be awkward. "Say, Melody, you can tell Jodi that as soon as I pass my solo flight I'll be able to give the two of you a ride."

"That will be great," she replied. "Grandmother sends her best. I've got to go now; supper is served. Thank you. I love you, Uncle Al."

"I love you, too, Melody." It was the first time she said that to him, and it warmed his heart. He turned to Lois Carson who was sitting at the kitchen table hulling strawberries they had picked that morning.

"Whenever you talk to the twins, a look of contentment comes over you, Al. I've missed that friendship I grew up with so many years ago."

"I often think back to those times, too, Lois. We've grown older, and maybe we see them as better than they actually were. When I met Meredith, she seemed to be the answer to all of my hopes and dreams. How badly I read my affection for her."

"She was never good for you, Al."

"I know that now, but it took a long time for reality to sink in. I always enjoyed seeing you and Carl together. I envied you two. You had much more compatibility than I did with Meredith."

"Oh, there were times when it wasn't all tea and roses." She got up to place the bowl of strawberries in the refrigerator. "I've got to run, Al. I promised Mother I'd be home before dark. She's a worry wart."

"You're good to her. Tell her that I'll give her a ride in the plane soon."

"I already have, and she's lukewarm about it," Lois laughed. "Thanks for a pleasant day." She embraced him and kissed him. "Until next time."

He walked her to the door. "Thanks for sharing the day with me. It's been nice. Drive carefully."

"Now you sound like Ma," she sighed playfully.

He watched her Nash Rambler turn out of the driveway and had returned to the kitchen for a cup of coffee. The quiet hush of a summer evening after the sun had set was a good time to evaluate the day and to plan for tomorrow. Lois had always been a positive element in his life. She was fun to be with and was more socially active than he ever was. She had been a true friend ever since they were together in Miss LeClair's first grade class. That friendship never varied even after she married Carl.

Carl had been one of Al's best friends. He came from a dysfunctional family that had been shattered by alcohol abuse with both parents. His father was a brutish alcoholic who forced Carl to do most of the work about the house. Carl never complained or talked about the abuse he had to tolerate. One day, he was late in arriving home because he had tried out for the cross country team with Al. His father had to split some wood for the kitchen stove and was angry that Carl did not hurry home to do his chores. His father began to beat him with his powerful fists. His mother remained in an alcoholic stupor. There was no one to protect the frightened young man. After being beaten almost to unconsciousness, Carl picked up a piece of wood and hit his father in the head with it, knocking him out.

Frightened at what he had done, Carl ran the mile to Al's home where his mother opened the door and screamed for Alvin and his father to come to help Carl. He was bleeding all over himself! Al's mother cleaned the wounds so that they did not become infected. Carl stayed with the Starr family until he graduated from high school. Then he immediately joined the Army. It was during the Great Depression when jobs were scarce. The Army was good for him. When he came home for his first furlough, he stayed with Al and courted Lois. They were married within the year. It was a good match. Alvin was his best man. Carl's parents boycotted the affair. They never had any children, Carl didn't want them. When Lois received word of his death, she was like a lost soul without Carl.

Over the years, Al wondered why Lois never remarried. The war had changed a lot of things. Monson began to lose citizens who found better opportunities in the outside world. Lois had gone to normal school in Portland and became a teacher in Monson teaching the fifth grade.

The night of the alumni reunion was the first that Alvin had attended since he graduated twenty-two years ago. Dressed in his uniform because he had not gone shopping for civilian clothes, he stopped to pick up Lois. She was dressed in a dark

41

blue dress which highlighted her natural blonde hair. She was very attractive.

"You look great, Lois. I'm glad you're going with me. I was having some doubts about attending. It's been a long time, and old memories are still very much alive..."

Lois kissed him on the cheeks. "That's all the more reason to go now, Al. Those old echoes from your past are not relevant now. You are very handsome in your uniform. Come, tonight is supposed to be fun. A lot of old friends will be glad to welcome you home."

The night had gone quickly for him. He had laughed and joked about old-time events. Lois was very popular among the alumni. She danced most of the slow fox-trots and waltzes with Al and was pulled on the dance floor by others for the fast steps. It had been a fun evening, and by midnight he was ready to leave. Images of Meredith had been with him part of the evening. Friends cautiously avoided talking about her, but she remained active in his imagination.

He was quiet on his way to Lois's home. She picked up on his mood and did not intrude on his reflections. "Thanks for taking me, Alvin. It was nice to see you laugh with the old gang. I understand your reluctance to talk about it, but at some time, you've got to bury those feelings that are still holding you prisoner. I tell you that as a friend who really cares for your happiness."

"I know that, Lois. I'm sorry. To be honest, I'm not unhappy. It's just that those old feelings went so deep it'll take a long time to work them out of my system," he replied.

"Tell me honestly, Alvin. Am I the one to help you forget the past, or am I a constant reminder of that past which still troubles you?"

"You ask what I can't answer, Lois. If that hurts, I'm sorry, but it's the truth. Forgive me."

She kissed him goodnight and walked into the house.

Alvin was pragmatic enough to be honest with himself. He was pleased that the transition from life in the Coast Guard to civilian status had gone better than expected. The future looked promising. His spirit of independence and self-reliance was always active. After he had redone the cabin with the help of a carpenter, he built an operations room off the deck where he had installed a powerful radio capable of reaching within his radius of two hundred and fifty miles on a tank of fuel. He had purchased a large wall map that included portions of Quebec, Maine, New Hampshire, and New Brunswick. There was a large circle in red that indicated his round trip limit. He located several hunting and fishing lodges near waterways that he could land on to service the lodges.

The day he received his license, he also registered his radio call signal to be "Golden Angel." He could hardly contain his enthusiasm to fly his own plane from Folsom's to Lily Bay. He drove to Monson to see if Lois was at home. She was mowing her lawn when he drove into the driveway. Lois lived in a small bungalow on the northern shore of Lake Hebron with large white pine trees sheltering the house from heavy winds. It was a lovely setting and she kept it neat and orderly.

Lois recognized his truck and wiped the sweat from her brow. "My, what a pleasant surprise," she exclaimed, walking towards him. She saw that he was all smiles. "Is this the day you've been waiting for, Al?"

"It is," he replied, holding the license for her to see. "Now I can fly my plane anywhere legally."

She embraced him. "Congratulations! This calls for a celebration. I've got some ice cold lemonade in the fridge. Will you join me in a toast to your elevated status?"

"It'll be my pleasure. You're the first to know. I have a favor to ask of you."

She led him into the kitchen. "I'm always available for an old friend." She poured two glasses of lemonade and ice cubes. Passing one to him she looked into his eyes. "If your new license and airplane are responsible for putting the gleam in your eyes, then I want to be the first to drink a toast to them. I'm glad for you, Al."

"I want to move my plane from Folsom's to my dock at Lily Bay. Would you drive my truck from Greenville to Lily Bay while I fly the plane?"

"I will on one condition. I must be the first passenger to ride with you. Is it a deal?" she teasingly asked.

"You drive a hard bargain, Lois. It's a deal," he said, lifting his glass to her. "My friend, Carl, chose wisely."

The moment of intimacy brought tears to her eyes. She lifted her glass and said, "Touché."

He lifted a strand of blonde hair from her cheek and gently kissed her. She placed her glass of lemonade on the counter and embraced him. "Is this for real, Al?"

"It seemed to be the right thing to do, Lois," he replied, cautiously choosing his words.

She reached up to touch his face with her soft fingers. "You never knew it, but my world collapsed when I heard that you had married Meredith. Carl and I had a wonderful marriage, and I loved him. At the same time, you, my friend, always occupied a very special place in my heart that was never replaced. To be really honest, I'm a little overwhelmed by this moment and a little frightened at the same time."

Over the years, Alvin had surmised the feelings she had confessed, but he was too involved with the turmoil in his own life to pay much attention to an old friend's private emotions. He released her and said, "Lois, for a long time I've been looking for something that would give my life more meaning. After Meredith's unfaithfulness and ensuing death, I saw every woman that came near me as a threat to my sanity. It's been a lonely road until I came home and started to build a new life outside of the Coast Guard. Your wonderful positive outlook on life has been a healing experience for me. Our friendship has been a stabilizing and meaningful factor like sailing into calm waters. I have to add that the twins, Jodi and Melody, have also been a rewarding experience to me. What do you say if we build on our foundation of friendship and see what tomorrow brings? I know that does not answer your question, but I'd like to think that an old friend will understand my position."

She was disappointed, but was able to accept his honest answer. "Yes, dear friend. Tomorrow never looked so promising..."

Chapter Six

The summer Alvin obtained his license turned out to be more profitable and busier than he had anticipated. He flew countless sight-seeing trips around the Moosehead Lake region. August was proving to be a very dry month, so the Maine Forest Service stepped up his fire patrol flights to extend to the Canadian border along the Allagash Wilderness Waterway. Whenever possible he accepted two or three passengers to accompany him on the patrol. The extra eyes were responsible for spotting a few more fires.

Occasionally he had located fires on the Canadian side and duly called them in to the Canadian authorities. He was licensed to travel into Canadian air space with sportsmen to hunt or fish and to supply their camp. Those were the most profitable flights. He had equipped the Beaver with every navigational aid on the market suitable for an aircraft. Navigation was a science in which he was well trained by the Coast Guard. He wanted his plane to have the same capabilities as the patrol boats of the Coast Guard. He was not a strong believer in flying by the "seat of his pants" solely by visible land marks.

One addition to the Beaver that pleased him more than anything else was to arrive at a suitable name for the aircraft. He had searched for a local artist that was capable of capturing the image he carried in his head of the little girl that had drowned in the North Atlantic while he looked on helplessly. He found a man from Shirley who had been an Army medic in World War Two. Alvin described in detail what had taken place. He wanted an ethereal atmosphere as a background with the blond little girl's image superimposed on cumulus clouds looking upward with her right hand reaching out for him to help her.

It was a challenging image for any artist to attempt, but the veteran medic, who had seen death and devastation close up on the battlefield, had witnessed similar scenes and did a pencil drawing for Alvin's approval. The minute Alvin looked at the drawing he cried aloud: "You've got it right, Roger. The eyes are as I remembered them, and the outstretched tiny fingers reaching for me is perfect. Can you duplicate this in colors on both side of the cowl on my plane?"

"I'm sure I can, Alvin," replied Roger in his quiet way. "Are you sure you want to be reminded of her every time you climb into the cockpit of the plane?"

"I do this as a remembrance of a lost soul. By taking her portrait up into the sky, maybe she'll be happy that someone remembers her in a special way. I don't do this for me; I do it for her."

"I'm honored to create this for you, Al. It will also help me put to rest a lot of ugly images I still hold from the beaches of Normandy," Roger replied.

"The uniforms we wore demanded a lot from us. Welcome aboard, Roger. I'm going to be proud to take *Golden Angel* with me whenever I lift from Mother Earth and touch the face of God."

The artwork was a reflection of the portraits that members of the Eighth Air Force fashioned on their bomber noses. Al was pleased to be carrying on an honored tradition.

Shortly after the art work was completed, the twins and Merci made their first visit to his log cabin. The very first thing they did upon arrival was to take a ride in the airplane. He circled the lake and dropped down low to the water for a better look of the sheer cliff at Kineo. He told them that the large hotel that had burned on the top of the cliff had a steam-powered elevator that ran up and down the face of the cliff.

At first the twins were scared, but soon were preoccupied watching the people and places below that looked very small from their perspective in the air. Merci sat up front with him, enjoying the ride. She saw a level of contentment on Alvin's face that was not always present. He had not said anything about the *Golden Angel* name for the plane. She looked at it as she was climbing into the cockpit, but did not comment.

Once they landed and secured the plane to the dock, Merci told the twins they could change into their suits for a swim.

"There are two bedrooms in the cabin where you two can change. I'll fire up the grill while you two take a dip in the water. It's quite warm today."

"What's the significance of such a unique name for your plane, Chief?" Merci asked, studying the portrait.

He turned to Merci and said, "The name on my plane, *Golden Angel,* has a very specific meaning for me. It's difficult to explain. I don't expect anyone to understand why I chose that name." He avoided her inquiring glance, pausing to say, "Let me tell you a story, and then maybe you can better understand what it means for me."

With that introduction, Alvin described the rescue operation of the burning yacht when he saw a little girl, four or five years old with blonde curly hair, trapped in the tangled wreckage of the ship sink beneath the water. Her last frightening words were "Mommy...Mommy..."

"I touched her fingers as she was pulled from my grasp. I often hear her small terrified voice in my dreams. In some small way I've felt guilty. She was my responsibility, and I lost her to the cold depths of the water below..."

"You did all that mortal man could do, Chief. The loss of that little girl may be hard to understand, but surely you cannot be blamed for the tragedy. My faith tells me that God had plans for her and took her home. We have to accept His wishes." She saw that her comforting words had triggered a response. He turned away from her to hide the moisture collecting in his eyes.

Merci walked closer to the plane and studied the portrait. It was then that she discovered the sad, forlorn look in the eyes of the little girl. It touched her. "The artist certainly captured the poignancy and terror of the moment. It's truly a work of art."

He continued to look away and walked to the edge of the dock, looking across the water. "I had the hope that wherever that precious soul is now, just maybe she would see the plane and know that someone remembers her and would like for her to know that I'm sorry that I was too late to save her. I had a feeling on my first flight, after the paint had dried, that she was with me and understood. That has pleased me, for it would be a double tragedy if such a beautiful human being was lost forever in the struggle for survival. I apologize for my emotional remembrances.

"I hope she approves of my actions. She's been a part of my life ever since that night in the North Atlantic. I'm not sure if I did it for her or for myself, but it's done, and I've found some comfort since it was completed."

Merci laid her hand on his arm. "I did not mean to ask hurtful questions. I think it's a wonderful gesture on your part to pay tribute to the memory that is such a sacred part of your past. My friend, Chief Petty Officer Alvin Starr, has exposed a part of his soul for all the world to see. How nice it is that a strong man possesses such compassion. Today I've seen what the twins perceived in you the first time we met on the road."

Alvin blew his nose and turned to her. "Thanks for understanding. Your approval of my intentions is important to me."

"Thank you for sharing your thoughts with me, Alvin." She embraced him and held him in her arms. "At some time, dear friend, you've got to stop living in the past."

It was a solemn moment for both of them. "You're not the first person to tell me that, Merci," he replied. "Merle is a lucky man to have won your heart."

She released him and was about to reply when the twins came running from the cabin with their bathing suits on. Jodi loved the water and leaped off the end of the dock, curling into a ball before he hit the water. Melody was still uncertain about ducking her head and slowly waded from the sandy shore into the water beside the dock gangplank.

Merci insisted that Jodi swim around so that he could be with Melody who had just this summer begun to swim alone. Alvin had an inner tube and threw it into the water.

"I have some fresh trout I caught yesterday. Would you and the twins be my guests for lunch?" he asked Merci.

"That would be nice. I haven't had fresh trout in ages. Is there anything I can do to help?" she asked, watching the twins play ball in the water.

"I also have some string beans and small potatoes fresh from the garden. They'll take a little longer to cook, so I'll start the grill now. It's great to have company. As soon as the twins come out of the water, they can change in the bedrooms. I'll show you my operations room off the deck of the cabin. I've finally got it set up the way I want it."

"You've been a busy man since we first met, Chief. Do you miss the Coast Guard?"

"I'll always miss the camaraderie that exists in the Coast Guard. They are the most devoted men I've ever encountered in my forty-one years. I'll go put on my chef's hat now," he started up the gangplank and turned to her. "Make yourself comfortable, Merci."

"We'll be in shortly, Chief. Melody starts to shiver when she's in the water too long. Thanks for being such a nice host."

By the time Alvin started the charcoal, Merci herded the twins into the cabin. Melody was wrapped in a large towel with her teeth chattering.

Alvin smiled at her. "A lot of people react that same way to the cool waters of Moosehead, Melody. I've got the string beans and potatoes on boiling. We'll wait a few minutes before grilling the trout. I'll show you my hobby room. Some would call it a war room or an operations room. I like to think of it as my study. It makes it sound more impressive than a radio room."

Merci followed him into the sunny room with a southwestern view that captures the sun for most of the day. Against one wall Alvin had installed a powerful radio capable of reaching a hundred miles beyond the fuel limit of his plane. A large table held a typewriter and lamps that lit the entire communication area. The rear wall opposite the large window was filled from top to bottom with a large map that was lit with fluorescent lights at the top of the wall. They lit up the full map without any shadows. He told her that the light green circle at the center of the map represented the circumference limit of round-trip travel for his plane without refueling. It went into Quebec and New Brunswick as well as Vermont and New York.

The wall opposite the radio center was his private library filled with books of every description on navigation, seamanship, meteorology, and a varied number of novels by Zane Gray, James Oliver Curwood, and others.

"I've recently been impressed by a Canadian author, Farley Mowat, who recently wrote *PEOPLE OF THE DEER* and *THE DESPERATE PEOPLE*. He's a beautiful writer with a passion

49

and the courage to defy Canada's policies for the northern native communities. I'm a fan."

Merci checked out the extent of his library and was impressed. "You've accumulated a large number of books," she exclaimed approvingly, noting the comfortable chair and reading lamp placed in front of the bookcase. "I've heard of Farley Mowat. He's quite popular with some of the faculty members at the university. What is the significance of the red pins and the green pins on the map?"

"The green ones," he said, pointing to one near the Canadian border, "represent fishing groups that I have dropped off and need to be picked up or supplied with food. Every party that has been inserted into the wilderness is registered by me at Folsom's Airways so that if something happens to me, the party will not be left stranded. The red pins are near ponds or waterways that are too dangerous to land my Beaver. Most are simply too shallow in the drought season."

She quietly asked if she could be excused to a private place where she could administer an insulin shot. "This disease is my reality check every day."

"Of course, Merci," he replied, gently taking her by the arm, leading her to the bathroom off the great room at the center of the cabin. "Your friends and the twins understand your responsibility to take good care of yourself. I like to think I'm one of those friends."

"You're very generous, Chief. There are those who are not as kind, thank you."

Chapter Seven

Alvin had a surprise for the last course, homemade coffee ice cream. He had cooked the mixture and chilled it overnight. He poured the mixture into the steel canister of the White Mountain ice cream maker.

Ice alternated with a covering of rock salt was poured around the canister in the wooden freezer, then Alvin began to slowly turn the crank that rotated the canister within the ice and salt mix. He had a large smile on his lips and placed a pillow on the top of the freezer's gear mechanism and invited Melody to sit on it so as to hold it from moving around on the back step of the cabin. Jodi was given a chance to turn the handle and thought it was too hard. Alvin tried it and told them it was definitely thickening, but they would turn it for five more minutes to be sure.

They uncapped the cranking gears and removed the cap of the canister containing the ice cream. Merci was ready with a large bowl to receive the wooden ladle covered with fresh made ice cream. The twins were given the ladle to spoon it off. They licked every morsel from it. The ice cream was a hit with everybody. Alvin realized that Merci could not overindulge on the sweet dessert, but the twins ate more than he expected, which pleased him.

Merci had enjoyed herself and was especially pleased the way her grandchildren interacted with Alvin. He thought she was quieter than usual. Melody had asked him to play the piano. She had looked at some of the sheet music he had on the instrument. He sat down and ran through several of the popular songs of the period: *Yellow Rose of Texas, Davy Crockett, Sixteen Tons,* and *Harbor Lights,* his favorite. Merci recognized it and listened closely.

51

"That song is one of my favorites, Chief. I know it's awful to eat and run, but we've got to get back to Alton. Thanks for being such a good host. We've enjoyed the plane ride and the day with you. Come children, get your bathing suits on the drying line."

The twins embraced Alvin as he kneeled to hold them in his arms. "Thank you for the fun day, Uncle Al," Jodi said. Before Merci and the twins left for Bangor, everybody had pitched in to clean up after the meal.

Melody had been her usual quiet self during the visit. Alvin was aware of her reflective observance of everything around her. She was a serious child who cultivated his instinctive desire to shelter her from hurtful situations. She had sensed that about him since their first encounter on the road, and embraced him, whispering in his ear: "Someday I'm going to play the violin as good as you do the piano. I love you, Uncle Al."

Her soft voice touched him, and he kissed her on the forehead. "I'm sure you'll exceed my skills, Melody. I'm glad that you like your music lessons. I love you and Jodi, too. Since you've been a part of my life, things have gone well for me. Thanks for coming. I promise to see you again soon. Take good care of Grandmother."

She grabbed her bathing suit from Jodi, and the two climbed into the front seat of the Studebaker.

Alvin turned to Merci with a serious expression on his face and waited until Melody and Jodi were out of hearing distance. "Thanks for coming. It's not my way to butt into other people's business, Merci, but you've been a little more reflective today than usual. Is there anything I've done or that a friend can help you with? If you tell me that I should mind my own business, I'll understand."

"You've done nothing but make this a good day, Chief. If you don't mind, I choose not to answer your question, but thanks for the offer to help. I value our friendship very much. We're proud to see how settled and organized your life has become. It's nice to see you so happy. Thanks for everything. Good-bye, Chief."

She kissed him on the cheek and they walked to the Studebaker where he opened the door for her to get behind the wheel. She smiled at him and drove the car out of the driveway. As soon as the taillights disappeared, loneliness enveloped him.

That evening, he received a call from a man in Bar Harbor who was inquiring about hiring him to take a fishing party of four adults into a remote lake near the Canadian border. He told the man that his plane could hold that kind of a load, passengers and their luggage, and was limited to landing on waterways that accepted float planes.

The next day he woke to a clear, sunny day with low winds, perfect for flying. He first stopped at Folsom's for fuel and signed a flight plan with the radio dispatcher. An hour later he landed in Frenchmen's Bay between Acadia National Park and Winter Harbor on the east shore of the mainland. He was directed to a landing dock where the four adults and their luggage were waiting. He shut the engine down and jumped on the dock to secure the plane.

"I'm Alvin Starr," he announced, offering his hand to the man who greeted him.

"I'm George Harris, the man who called you, Mr. Starr. Your airplane is just right..."

George was interrupted by a frantic call over the radio: "Mayday...mayday... can anyone hear me?"

Alvin leaped into the cockpit to respond to the call. "This is *Golden Angel* at Bar Harbor. I read you and have your transponder locked into my homing beacon. Is there anyone else responding to this mayday call? Repeat, is anyone responding to call for help?" No one was answering!

"Mayday... mayday, our boat is burning, and we are abandoning ship into two life boats. We have life preservers for all..."

"Leave your radio on when you leave the craft for the lifeboats. Where are you in relation to Bar Harbor? How far out to sea are you from the Maine coast? Repeat...how far are you from the mainland?"

"Our best estimate is thirty to forty miles... the ship is sinking rapidly..."

Alvin quickly set his homing beacon on the weak signal remaining. It quickly went dead, but he had the correct azimuth to locate the position. "I'm sorry, Mr. Harris, but I must respond to cries for help. No one else has picked up the mayday signal. I'm sorry... I'll return as quickly as I can."

"Calls for assistance on the ocean are serious, and you are correct in responding. We commend your attitude, sir."

"Today someone else is in harm's way. Tomorrow it may be me," Alvin said, starting the engine and slamming the powerful Pratt and Whitney rotary engine to full throttle. Once he was airborne, he got on the phone to locate more assistance. "Mayday, mayday, Coast Guard, do you read me?"

"This is the Coast Guard cutter *Reliance,* we are reading you loud and clear."

"This is *Golden Angel* responding to a mayday off the Bar Harbor coast. A ship of unknown type has caught fire and is sinking as we speak. Survivors have two lifeboats. I'm responding with a float Beaver aircraft on an azimuth I picked up before it went dead. My help will be limited. Can you assist me?"

"We cannot help you until we have removed all passengers from a ferry that has gone aground in Casco Bay. Our best ETA to your location would be three to four hours. Good luck *Golden Angel.*"

"Roger and Out," Alvin replied. He knew that they had their hands full and would respond quickly when free of their current rescue mission.

"*Golden Angel* this is Marine Patrol out of Bar Harbor. We have been monitoring your conversation with *Reliance.* We are following your signal and are underway with a forty foot patrol launch. ETA is one hour at most. We're receiving a clear signal from you. Keep your radio on this frequency and keep us posted when you arrive at the crash scene."

"Thanks, Marine Patrol. Roger and out."

He dropped to a low altitude just off the churning Atlantic waters so that he could pick up the site and the debris field easier. He prayed that the survivors of the sinking ship were not lost and that he could get there in time to at least give moral support to the people alone and frightened in the dark ocean. Visibility was good. That was a blessing, but the sea was filled with heavy swells that had the capacity to sink a float plane if it was hit on the side by a big swell.

Twenty minutes after losing the signal, he saw two lifeboats in the middle of a dispersed debris field. He immediately described the scene below to Marine Patrol, knowing that the Coast Guard was also monitoring all calls. The two life boats were filled to capacity with a few people in the water hanging to the sides of the boats.

Alvin circled close to the water above the boats and turned on his loudspeaker: "I will land and approach you at an idle. Do not leave your boats and approach the plane for now. I can take a few passengers in the cabin. Women and children first up to seven people. Then I want you to carefully attach your lifeboats to my floats with a rope I will throw to you. I have two rubber inflatable rafts that I will also throw to you for the people in the water. Do you understand me?"

An arm lifted out of the water waving an orange flag. The man gave him a thumbs up signal that he understood. "I see you, sir. Please keep your people from climbing on the floats." He stopped the engine, climbed out on the float and threw a mooring rope. A man in the boat caught the rope and pulled the plane and boat closer. Then Alvin threw two rafts into the water. They immediately inflated with a bang.

Alvin was standing on the float with his preserver on and told the anxious people; "I'm Alvin Starr. I picked up your weak signal for help. I should tell you that additional help is on the way to you. In the meantime, please place all of the children you have in the rubber rafts. I'll put them inside of the plane. How many are in your group?"

"We have four small children, six women and twenty men. I'm Captain Smith. We were lucky we all survived a fire at sea."

"I'll take three women with the children inside the plane. The rest of you will have to remain in the boats and rafts until the Marine Patrol arrives. Be patient. We'll have you back in port soon," he said, lifting the children from the raft into the cabin. "Don't be afraid, children, and you, too, ladies. You're getting the best seats in the house. One of the adults can sit up front with me. Would you ladies see that all of the children fasten their seat belts? And that goes for you, too."

Once the cabin was filled, Alvin turned to Captain Smith. "Are you ready to proceed, Captain?"

"Yes, sir. All of our people have life preservers on. We're ready. Thank God you heard our call."

"I'm an old Coast Guard hand. I could not ignore a mayday call. Tomorrow it may be me calling you."

"How true, sir. The sea is unforgiving."

"Okay. Now I'm going to start the plane and will pull you towards Bar Harbor. I have to warn you that no float plane can survive swells such as we now have if they hit sideways of the floats. I will head straight into the swells and ride over them rather than have them slap against our side. Do not be afraid and hold onto the boats and rafts. Before you know it, we'll be in sight of Mount Desert. If you have a problem and want me to stop, Captain, shoot this flare gun to my left." He tossed the loaded flare gun to the Captain in one of the rubber rafts.

"Marine Patrol calling *Golden Angel*. How much fuel do you have aboard?"

"I have enough to return to Winter Harbor. Thanks for asking. The entire crew and passengers of the burned ship are now in tow and heading for port. Your arrival will lighten our load, out."

Several large swells had almost overturned the boats in tow behind the plane. Alvin had a difficult time steering the plane. The swells rolled towards the west so that they hit the boats before they arrived under the floats. If he was not exact in his positioning of the plane and boats, the boats frequently were hit from the side by the swells. It was a dangerous thing, but there was nothing that could be done. If the boats were left motionless in the water, they would be in more danger. The steady tension on the line to pull them forward helped to stabilize them to some degree. Alvin actually had better control if he increased speed so that the nose of the floats partially lifted out of the water.

The Marine Patrol launch was in sight about an hour after Alvin took the boats under tow. It was a welcome sight for everybody, Alvin included. He cut the engines and climbed out on the left float. He saluted the young sergeant who was commander of the craft. "To say that we are happy to see you is an understatement, Sergeant."

The young officer returned his salute. "You've done a marvelous job of getting the people this far from the wreckage. I'm Sergeant Welch of the Maine State Police. We can take all of your passengers, Mister Starr. I've been in contact with the Coast Guard cutter *Reliance,* and one of your old buddies, Captain Andrew Neville, gives his regards and a 'well done' also. You Coasties are a unique breed. It's my pleasure to meet you, sir."

"I was only a chief about the same rank as you, Sergeant," he replied, passing the children to the eager hands on the launch. "It will be good to fly this plane again. It was a lousy handler in the high seas. These people have been through a bad experience and they have faced their misfortune with courage. I salute all of you."

The doughty Captain Smith had been pulled aboard the launch and he leaned over the side to shake his hand. "Mr. Starr, you have turned a disaster into a triumph of the human spirit. I cannot explain the feeling of thanksgiving that came over our troubled fellow passengers when we saw your plane circle our position. Thank you for your courage and skill in snatching us from potential death. May God chart your course."

"Thank you, Captain Smith," he replied, pulling his inflatables out of the water and unsnapping the air plug to collapse them. "By the way, Sergeant Welch, what are you going to do with the life boats?"

"I should take them ashore, but with this load, I'm going to sink them with gunfire. We don't want to leave a navigating hazard behind."

"I agree, Sergeant. Thanks for answering the call for help." Alvin shook his hand and pushed his plane from the side of the launch, starting the engines. He waved to the people on the launch as he lifted off the water on the top of a large swell.

Chapter Eight

Alvin returned to Winter Harbor to pick up his clients for a fishing trip in the Maine wilderness. He had been gone only three hours to aid in the rescue of thirty people - time well spent! He had placed himself and his new airplane in a dangerous situation that could have been disastrous with his limited experience as a pilot. The sturdy Beaver had performed magnificently and quite possibly had overshadowed any mistakes he had made in executing the rescue. Now that it was all over, he was concerned at what might have gone wrong and turned a rescue attempt into an even greater tragedy. It was his habit to evaluate his moves, and he was satisfied that he had acted prudently and would do the same things again if given the opportunity.

The stop at Winter Harbor was brief. The plane was filled to capacity with gasoline, and the fishing party was eager and ready to board for the flight to northern Maine. The four adults had selected a very isolated location to spend part of their vacations that summer. The most important thing, according to George Harris, was to get away from the hustle and bustle of New York City and ringing telephones. Square Lake was located about twenty miles south of the Canadian border in Aroostook County, Maine.

Access to the camping site was available only by float plane. A number of log cabins had been built on a stretch of land on the eastern shore. Alvin imagined that the owners had positioned the cabins so as to take advantage of the sunsets that can be beautiful in the more northern latitudes. The cabins were leased or rented for extended periods of time. They were serviced by a centrally located diesel-powered generator which gave the cabins running water, lights, and refrigeration. The modern facilities contributed to the enjoyment of an isolated location.

The sturdy Beaver was refueled again at Folsom's for the final leg into the northern wilderness that extended for miles into Quebec and New Brunswick, Canada. He liked flying in the remote regions. There was a quiet sense of peace that prevailed in the wilderness that he could not find elsewhere. He told the passengers that they were flying over land owned by the Great Northern Paper Company. The forest had been cut-over several times during the past century and a half. The famous Allagash wilderness region was not any different than the region they were going to be vacationing in.

Alvin surmised that George Harris and his wife, Elaine, were wealthy people. He owned a large construction company that specialized in building roads, bridges and airports. The other woman, Kimberly Lambert, was a sister to Elaine. She rode up front with Alvin. Elaine talked some with her sister but got a limited response from her. They all used the internal microphones in the cabin, enabling them to converse in normal tones. The fourth person, Sam Olson, was a partner in George's construction company.

Kimberly Lambert made no effort to converse with Alvin or anyone else in the plane. The others seemed pleased to be on their way to a well-deserved vacation to fish and relax. Alvin had signed a contract with George to fly into their location every three or four days, weather permitting, with supplies. He imagined that the lady's silence was from fear of flying. "Have you flown in a single engine plane before, Mrs. Lambert?" he casually asked to start a conversation.

"I've flown on commercial airlines several times. This is my first time in a small plane. The wilderness is very beautiful. My sister insisted that I make this trip with her."

He detected an air of reluctance and was not interested in getting into personal differences with his clients. He checked his watch and was thinking about his planned return to Lily Bay that evening. By the time they arrived and got the plane unloaded, it would be dusk with total darkness soon after. Nights in the wilderness were darker than anyone had ever witnessed in the civilized world. The wilderness was completely devoid of any light source except the moon, stars and the Aurora Borealis which is an experience beyond compare.

"George," Alvin announced, "it will be dark by the time we land and get you settled in the cabin. I'm going to sleep in the plane for the night."

"You're welcome to bunk in the cabin, Alvin. There should be plenty of room," George replied.

"Thanks just the same, but I prefer to stay with the aircraft. I'll fly out before sunrise. That's always a nice experience to see a new day give birth."

"Does your wife worry when you do not come home at night?"

"My wife passed away years ago," Al told him without getting into detail.

"If this outing does not work well for the ladies, would you be available to take them back to Winter Harbor?"

"Yes, if that's what they want. I have a forest fire patrol every other day," Alvin replied. "Do they have a radio transmitter at the cabins?"

"I believe so, Alvin. In the case of an emergency, who do we call?" George asked.

"Mayday Folsom's Airways. The dispatcher is a good friend, and he monitors all flights into the north country. Square Lake should be straight ahead," Alvin announced.

Suddenly, Kimberly Lambert turned in her seat to confront her sister. "Elaine, I don't think this is going to be right for me. I could go back with the pilot..."

"Kim, you know how hard we've worked, and you agreed to give this a chance." Elaine placed a comforting hand on Kimberly's shoulder and continued in a desperate tone, "now that we're together, I can't let you go again. Please, Kim, give us a chance."

"Oh, I do want that, Elaine, more than you can ever know. It's hard, and I'm afraid," she cried and turned back into her seat, weeping softly, folding and unfolding her hands repeatedly.

Alvin was a witness to an exchange that bothered him. The lady beside him was carrying a burden that was smothering her. He had actually sensed that the first time he saw her standing on the dock at Winter Harbor. She seldom smiled.

The lake came into view. "Square Lake is just ahead," he announced upon their arrival. "I'm going to make a low run over the landing area to check for logs or any other impediment that could damage a float. Be sure that your seat belts are secured. The water landing can be rough, but do not worry; it's normal."

He checked his front passenger. "Mrs. Lambert, would you please fasten your seat belt? We don't want you to be hurt."

He saw pain in her sad eyes. She buckled the belt as requested. As they turned at the northern end of the lake, they were a witness to a beautiful sunset off to the west. The setting sun was suspended on the peak of a mountain showering it in a red glow that reached down into the water of the lake.

Elaine reached for her sister and grasped her shoulder. "I think it's a good omen for you, Kim. Please, give us a chance..."

It was an intimate moment before he applied all of his attention and skill into making a soft landing on the lake. Water spouts spread out on each side of the aircraft as it settled into the water with the nose slightly elevated. He was pleased, as it was the best landing he had ever made. The dock jutted into the lake for a hundred feet. He gently nosed the plane close to it and killed the engine. The left float gently touched the dock when he leaped from the seat, securing the aircraft to a hitching post with a rope.

He opened the rear door and held the front door open for Kimberly. She avoided his inquiring eyes and stepped onto the dock, accepting his hand to steady herself. "Thank you," she said and was escorted off the landing by her sister Elaine and her husband.

Sam Olson offered to help Alvin remove the baggage from the storage compartment behind the passengers, placing it on the landing. Alvin closed the doors on the plane and helped Sam carry them to the closest cabin. They each made several trips, working up a sweat in the process. Sam was a man in his sixties in good physical condition. He was not one to talk a lot. "You're welcome to join us in a lunch of some kind," he said.

"I appreciate your offer, sir. It appears as if it would be more politic to let your party adjust to the cabin for the night without any interference from a stranger like me. I have several of the Army field rations that come in handy on occasions like this. I actually like them."

"I'm an old Army hand, Alvin. I swore when I left Okinawa that I would never touch one of those rations again. Over the years I've enjoyed their convenience on many a fishing trip," he laughed. "George told me that you're a Coast Guard veteran of twenty years."

"Yes, sir. A leg wound kept me from going to thirty. I'm thoroughly enjoying my retirement."

"Good for you, Alvin. I retired after thirty-five years in the Army. Now, I'm busier than ever. Fishing in remote waters is one of my passions. I'm afraid I'm the one who talked George and his wife and her sister into making this excursion," Sam told him.

They made three trips each to carry the luggage into the cabin. The diesel generator had kicked in, giving the cabin plenty of light. Alvin bid all of them a pleasant experience in the seclusion of the Maine woods. "The loons will be a treat for you tonight. Their melancholic call never ceases to remind me how insignificant we really are. It's a great reality check. Well, goodnight to all of you. I hope I don't wake you when I take off early morning. I'll see you again in a few days. Enjoy the fishing."

Alvin folded the rear seats out of the way and spread a couple of blankets on the floor to sleep. He used an inflated pillow to rest his head. Before he turned in, he collected a pipe and tobacco from one of the compartments in the pilot's door and sat on the landing dangling his feet above the water, lighting a pipe. He was not a habitual smoker, but one always appealed to him in the solitude of the wilderness. His first conscious movement was to search out the heavens for the North Star. It was the only star in the galaxy that did not move and has been a guiding force for mariners for ages. He always felt secure when he had oriented himself with it.

It was a beautiful night without a cloud in the sky. He felt comfortable with his light jacket on. The lake's location was several miles north of Quebec City. The nights could be cool. Loons were particularly active that night. They sent out their medieval call across the water, dominating the other voices of the wilderness. Alvin heard the closing of a door at the cabin and looked to see Kimberly Lambert watching the night skies. She stood motionless for several minutes and then walked directly to where he was sitting on the landing beside the plane.

"It's a beautiful evening, Mrs. Lambert," he said. "I heard you close the door at the cabin. I hope everything is satisfactory for you. These cabins have a reputation of living up to their advertisement."

"They are just fine, Mr. Starr," she said, holding a flashlight in her hand. "My sister said that you have a unique name on your plane. Is your radio call really *'Golden Angel'*?"

"Yes, it's true, Mrs. Lambert," he replied, thinking the question was strange. "The reason I used that call is very personal to me, and I'm proud to do so."

"May I see the picture on your plane that accompanies the name?"

"I have no reason to hide it from anyone. It has generated many sincere compliments from a large number of people. You may turn your light on the cowl of the plane if you wish."

She did as he suggested and carefully shown the light on the words 'Golden Angel' and then turned it onto the face of the child. She studied it for several seconds and cried out: "my God, it's Lee...it's Lee...." Then she collapsed on the landing.

Chapter Nine

Alvin saw her knees buckle in the dim light and rushed to her side. "Mrs. Lambert, what's wrong?" he asked, stunned by her words: "It's Lee... it's Lee..."

"Can you hear me, Mrs. Lambert? Please don't faint on me." He took off his jacket and gently placed it under her head. "Can you hear me? You're frightening me, Mrs. Lambert. Can you hear me?"

She lifted up on one elbow and said, "Yes, I hear you, and I apologize for my reaction. Would you please help me to stand up?"

"Are you sure?"

"Yes, it's just that your portrait on the plane reminded me of my daughter Lee.... It's amazing. I must be dreaming or going mad. How can it be??? You're a total stranger to me, yet... Would you please shine the flashlight on the little girl's face?"

Alvin was wondering if it was himself that was going mad. He picked up the flashlight from the dock and shined it on the little girl's face, holding the light as steady as he could.

Again, the lady softly kneeled and wept in her two hands. "I don't know if God is punishing me or not. Are my eyes deceiving me, or am I simply going mad, seeing things that are not real? Oh God help me, help me," she wept, shaking all over.

He placed his jacket around her shoulders, stupefied about what was taking place there on the dock in the middle of a vast wilderness. Was she a raving lunatic, or was she also unhinged? A simple portrait of a little girl had wrought havoc with two total strangers hundreds of miles from civilization. "What is going on?" he screamed to himself.

"Lady, let me get your sister to help you. I'm as confused as you are, and it's frightening to me," he stated forcefully in her ear.

"No, please, please, don't call my sister. She'll think it's just another of my mental lapses. I can assure you, Mr. Starr, that I am not mad." Her statement was more a plea for him to believe in her than a statement of fact.

"First of all, may I call you Kimberly? You can call me Alvin. Out here in the deep forest, Mr. and Mrs. seem out of place and awkward. If you'll sit quietly and tell me what significance you attach to the portrait on my plane, I'll truthfully tell you why I did the picture and selected the name. I'm not trying to hide anything from anyone, but I can honestly tell you that the painting represents a painful period in my life. Can you trust me to hold what you may divulge to me? You don't know me, but I swear to God that I will not voice a word that you tell me in confidence. Trust me, and I'll trust you, okay?"

"I do trust you... Alvin," she quickly replied in a more rational tone. She sat at the edge of the dock with her legs dangling above the water.

He sat beside her, anxious to hear what she had to say. "That's an accomplishment, Kimberly."

"To be brief, I lost my daughter, Lee, when she was four-and-a-half years old. Her tragic death contributed to my collapse, and I was in a mental hospital for one year. When I was discharged from the hospital, I was prepared to get on with my life, hoping that my conduct and accomplishments would be pleasing to my precious Lee. My memories of her are just as vibrant today as they were ten years ago.

"A few years after my release, my husband found greener pastures, leaving me for a younger, more attractive woman and also leaving me heavily in debt. I struggled night and day to pay off the debt and found that a drink here and there helped to ease the pain and grief. Soon the bottle consumed me and became the center of my tormented existence. I hated myself and what I was doing, yet I continued the addiction. It's not a pretty picture, Alvin."

"No person is perfect or without sin. Some loads are just too heavy for simple mortals to bear," Alvin added, feeling privileged that Kimberly, a complete stranger to him, felt at ease enough to share her darkest terrors. He admired the spirit and courage that supported her through such a horrible journey alone.

"I recently completed a detoxification program at a local hospital. It was either that or death from alcohol poisoning. I'm the main reason Elaine and George selected this fishing trip to help me find myself. I'm not so sure that I want to find myself. Which person am I? An alcoholic, a deranged woman, a one-time architect, or a lost soul who has no place in society?"

"God has a place for all of us. We just have to search for it," Alvin replied, listening to a troubled woman bare her soul to a stranger. He had contempt and admiration for her at the same time. Was he too unbalanced?

He knew from first-hand experience the trauma created by a child's death. He had been in that dark place for a long time. He understood the intensity of the grief the lady carried. "Kimberly, how long ago did your daughter die?"

"Ten years."

"How did she die? Was she sickly for a long time?"

"My God, no, she was killed in a tragic accident at sea when I took her with me in a friend's yacht. The ship caught fire and sunk with Lee trapped somewhere in the wreckage. I was out of my mind with fear. The boat was sinking, and I could not find her anywhere...,"she cried hysterically.

As Alvin listened to Kimberly's description of her daughter's death, old memories returned in a hurry. "How did you escape from the burning ship?"

"The Coast Guard boat came close beside the ship. I was thrown into the water where men in rubber rafts took me to safety," she answered between sobs.

"No, it can't be," he exclaimed to himself. "The chances of her tragedy being the same time and place was way beyond the realm of possibility." He was emotionally charged and was concerned that he was losing his mind. He fought that old guilt that had never set him free. Could it be that the little girl whose fingers he had touched was the Lee that Kimberly was describing?

Two souls, two strangers meeting in the vast wilderness discovered that they had met ten years ago during an incident they viewed from two perspectives. Was it really the same tragedy?? If it was not a miracle, it was a hateful act of a deranged God. Both individuals sat on the dock and prayed for release from the pain.

Kimberly was the first to break the overpowering silence. She saw the turmoil that had consumed Alvin sitting by her side on the dock. She reached out to console him. "I did not mean to upset you. Memories of dark moments are always painful. I've been selfish in thinking that I was the only one to suffer. Forgive me, Alvin Starr." Her words were comforting.

"You have nothing to apologize for. You must know that I was the one to throw you into the water. I was also the one who tried to get to your little Lee trapped in the wreckage that was sinking fast. I touched her little fingers, but she was pulled away from me. I was too late. Her last words as she was sinking into the water were, "Mommie... Mommie..." The nightmare has been constantly with me, and tonight it's just as vivid as that day ten years ago. Our meeting here in such an isolated place learning that we share a common emotional burden defies logic. The real miracle here tonight is that the portraits are a likeness to your daughter, Lee. I've always believed that miracles can happen."

Kimberly recalled being picked up by a Coast Guardsman and thrown from the cat-walk on the ship into the water. Once she was on board the patrol boat she frantically looked to see if Lee was on board. From that moment to the present her life had been dominated by fear and inadequacies. The discovery of Lee's likeness on the plane reinforced her faith in a just God. The act had to have been Divine Intervention. There was no other logical explanation. At the same time, she learned that she was not the only one to suffer from the loss.

Alvin sat beside Kimberly and wiped the sweat from his brow. For the first time in ten years, the pain of failure was easier to bear. The cathartic exchange between Alvin and Kimberly had purged much of the anger and guilt he held inside. He looked up at the heavens alive with aurora borealis colors and designs streaking about in the sky. It was almost as if the God of the north wind, Boreas, was sending them a message of hope. His first thought, seeing the colorful display above, was that his intent to show a little girl, who had touched his heart, that she was not forgotten had been accomplished.

Kimberly reached out to take his hand and whispered what he had been thinking. "Thank you, God, for making this possible... thank you..."

He squeezed her hand, awed by the emotional experience they had shared.

The solemnity of the moment had been broken by George walking down the path to the landing with a flashlight in his hand. "It's a beautiful night, isn't it?" George announced himself to them. "I came out to watch the northern lights. They're a rare treat to those of us who do not live in the northern latitudes."

"Tonight's display is especially striking," Alvin acknowledged.

"I also wanted to ask you to bring us some fresh milk when you return in a few days. I completely forgot to add it to our list."

"I'll be glad to do that, George," Alvin replied.

"How are you doing, Kim? Your sister and I have been looking forward to this excursion with you. I hope this place is not too isolated for you."

"George, you've been a very patient and kind brother-in-law," she said, standing beside him. "Your planning for this outing has been perfect. I have something important to share with you and Elaine when I return to the cabin."

"Are you sure you don't want to bunk inside, Alvin? There's plenty of room for you."

"I appreciate the offer, George, but I prefer to stay with the plane. I'll be leaving at first break of day. Tonight has been a new awakening for me and I hope for Kimberly. She can explain that to you and your wife."

George sensed that something special had taken place. "Elaine and I will look forward to what you have to say. It sounds positive, and that will make all of us happy. Goodnight, and 'bon voyage,' Alvin. We'll be awaiting your return in a couple of days."

"Goodnight, George."

They watched him walk to the cabin. Kimberly turned to face Alvin. Flickering light and shadows shone on her face. "I would never have made it this far without George and Elaine. They'll be relieved when I tell them what we've discovered tonight. Hopefully, it will direct me to a new path filled with hope and resolution."

"I almost passed this trip over to the Folsom's. Now I know that it had to be fate or destiny which made it possible for me to take it. Before you go into the cabin, let me say that your long journey in purgatory has been a testament to the power of the human spirit. Your dedication to a little girl's memory has coincided with my own tribute. Lee has been a part of my life for these past years. Now she's at peace, and we can be assured that she will be pleased to watch her mother be happy and filled with hope for a better future. Her memory deserves that of you."

"You're a very kind person, Alvin. Thank you for being so supportive. Little Lee was a very special little girl. I'm sure she's happy where she is now. Your faithfulness to her memory is something that has released the chains that held me in bondage in dark places. Thank you for that."

"May I walk you back to the cabin?"

She linked her arm in his, and they slowly walked up the pathway. She kissed him on the cheek and entered the log cabin.

Chapter Ten

Alvin took off at dawn when the first rays of light hit the water, traveling west away from the cabin so as to not disturb them any more than was necessary. The area between the Canadian border and Moosehead Lake was an unbroken forest wilderness punctuated with pond and streams. He marveled at the sight of Ripogenus Dam with hundreds of cords of spruce and fir pulpwood floating in the large lake behind the dam. The sluiceway was open with pulpwood tumbling down the chute towards the Great Northern Paper Company's mill at Millinocket, Maine. He landed at Lily Bay and went to his operations room to check with his phone answering service. He had covered about a hundred miles in less than two hours since leaving Square Lake.

He was scheduled the next day to conduct a fire patrol for the Maine Forest Service and to leave supplies at a fishing party at Chesuncook Lake. That afternoon he fixed a meal of baked beans and brown bread, a long time favorite. They were a staple food in his childhood years. He had just cleaned the dishes in the sink when Lois pulled into the driveway.

She carried a basket of boulla rolls to the kitchen. They were a very special delicacy in the town of Monson among the Finnish and Swedish families. It was a sweet heavy bread with cardamom seeds. Alvin had a real liking for them and never got enough. It was a natural with coffee.

"Hi, stranger," he greeted her at the door, opening it for her to enter. "I can smell those rolls already."

"Mother made a batch, so I stole some of them to remind you of your roots in Monson," she smiled, placing the basket on the table.

"Will you join me in a coffee and a delicious sweet bite?"

70

"I was hoping you'd ask," she laughed.

"Why don't we have it out on the deck? I'll bring the coffee when it's ready."

Lois's visit was a great way to end the day. Her spontaneity had not changed. They talked about goings on in town. She told him of an offer she had to teach school at Wells, Maine, down on the coast and was uncertain if she should take it or not. "The school board in Monson is having trouble meeting expenses and is doubling several of the classes. I would find that difficult, and it's not fair to the children."

"Let's be honest, Lois. Monson is a town we both love because we grew up when it was a vibrant community. Our nostalgic attachment to the town overlooks many things. The town is slowly fading away. Once the slate quarries closed down, it was the beginning of the decline. Those of us who have had a chance to see the outside world can see that. Wells may be a good choice for you, Lois. What about your mother?"

"She thinks the same as you. I'm more concerned about being a long ways from you. You've built a firm foundation for yourself here in Lily Bay. If I was to take the job, I'd miss you. Would you miss me?"

"Of course, what a question! Say, I forgot to pick up my mail. Let's work off some of those boulla rolls we just ate."

She placed an arm around him and walked to the mail box at the end of the driveway. It was packed full of mail. "Don't you check it every day?" she asked good-naturedly.

"To be honest, I don't get much mail, and I've been up north for two days," he replied, thumbing through the envelopes. A thick envelope from Merci was on the top, and he opened it to find several snapshots of the twins and Merci. "Here are some pictures of the two kids and their grandmother that I met on the road coming home. I've mentioned them to you."

She studied them. "They're lovely children. Their grandmother has a rather sober air about her."

"She's a librarian at the University of Maine," he added.

"Do you see them often? The little girl looks a little withdrawn."

"You're a very perceptive person, Lois. She's a quiet kid. Yes, I'd say she's a little bit withdrawn. I've told you about their

71

mother. Merci, their grandmother, is good for them. They're lucky to have her."

"Well, Alvin, it's getting late. It's been nice seeing you again."

"Thanks for the boulla rolls and company. Say hi to your mother, for me."

She briefly kissed him on the lips and headed for her car, waving as she left the driveway. He went into the house and saw that she had forgotten her purse. A paperback book had fallen out on the table. He curiously picked it up. The title of the book, *TEARS IN THE DARKNESS,* by Kimberly Lambert, shocked him.

Lois drove back into the yard and rushed to the kitchen. "I forgot my purse."

"Yes, I saw it on the table and looked at the book you're reading."

"It's a powerful story by an excellent writer. The author, Kimberly Lambert, has written several bestsellers. This is her best one. I have a hard time putting it down. I'm off again. Bye, Al."

"Good-bye, Lois. Drive carefully," he smiled. "I know, just like your mother."

Anxious to obtain a copy of her book, Alvin's first thought was that the Greenville Library might still be open. He jumped into his truck and found it open. Rushing to the card catalogue he looked up Kimberly Lambert and found that the library had three volumes she had authored. *TEARS IN THE DARKNESS* was one of them. He had a card for the library and asked the librarian if the volume was available. She left the counter for several minutes and returned with a paperback copy. She told him that the book was a favorite for several months when it first came out a year ago. He purchased a copy at a local bookstore.

That night he read until midnight when he placed the book on his bedside table and shut off the light. It was, as Lois described, a powerful book filled with experiences that only one who has been there could describe. The fictitious story was revealing. Without question the suffering of the heroine in a state hospital and later addiction to alcohol was Kimberly's story. She did not hold back from telling about untold eruptions in her family and social life. Kimberly was a good writer who told her story in simple declarative sentences with a minimum of adjectives which made her storyline more compelling.

He turned off the light to get a good night's sleep. He was committed for a fire patrol flight of six hours or so. He thought about the other books Kimberly had written prior to her mental decline. They were historical novels about the Benedict Arnold trek through the Maine wilderness to attack Quebec in 1775 and another about the famous defeat of General Braddock's British regiment by the French in the French and Indian War.

The next day was clear and warm, perfect flying weather. He spotted two suspicious plumes of smoke and duly reported them to the central fire tower at Greenville on Squaw Mountain. Later that night, he finished the book. The ending was like a Greek tragedy; the heroine died an early death. Alvin tried to visualize what Kimberly looked like and was unable to recall her facial features. The evening of their discovery was dark, and prior to that she went out of her way to be distant and uncommunicative.

By noon he was securing the plane to the dock at Square Lake. He had supplies previously ordered along with mail, extra newspapers, and milk. He also had in his pocket a copy of one of her historical novels, *DEATH OF A REGIMENT*. He had found it on the shelf of the small Greenville bookstore.

George Harris met him at the landing dock. "You're right on time, Alvin. We were about ready to sit down to a lunch of fried trout. Will you please join us?"

"I'll be glad to, George. I haven't had fried trout in ages. I'll get your stuff out of the cargo area. The outfitters sent two gallons of milk."

"I missed my milk," George laughed, grabbing an armful of boxes and heading for the cabin. Alvin followed him.

Elaine opened the door for them. "You're a welcome sight, Alvin. We heard your plane before you circled the lake. Has George invited you to a trout lunch, or do you still call it dinner?"

"I'm of the old school, Ma'am. I still call it dinner and the evening meal supper. Old traditions die hard with me. George and I will have to make one more trip to get all of your supplies."

73

"Sam is off visiting with some other fishing party on the east shore of the lake," George told him as they were carrying the last of the supplies into the cabin.

Alvin was anxious to see Kimberly. Two days ago the two of them had shared emotions that affected their individual lives. He had been strengthened by the revelation and hoped that she had found some level of peace. The release and acknowledgement of the demons that had controlled both of them had to be empowering and a relief that it had taken place. He looked for her and saw that Elaine had set the table for four people. If Sam was away, then the fourth had to be for Kimberly. He had her book in his jacket pocket and wanted her autograph.

"These cabins are really nice," he declared. "I built a log cabin for myself at Lily Bay."

George entered the great room, which was the kitchen and dining room combined, with an armful of wood. "A fire feels good at night. I could take this kind of life without a complaint. Have a seat, Alvin. Make yourself at home. I've been fishing and have caught more than we can eat while they're fresh. Elaine suggested that I ease off," he smiled. Alvin liked the man.

Elaine was a petite natural blonde with an easy-going disposition. She joked easily with her husband. Unpretentious and straightforward, the couple were devoted to each other. George was short and stocky with powerful arms and an easy disposition. Alvin could readily picture him as an excellent heavy equipment operator on a construction site. His construction company had been very successful with the recent completion of a new four-lane highway from Kittery to Portland, Maine.

Kimberly walked into the room searching for Alvin. She was as anxious to see him as he was to see her. She was dressed in a light blue shirt with jeans and a pair of leather moccasins on her feet. She wore her natural blond hair pulled back from her ears to fall loose about her shoulders. She was not a beautiful woman, but there was something about her eyes that reflected the difficult road she had been traveling. She was slightly taller and heavier than her sister. Both had a wholesome air about them.

"It's nice to see you again, Alvin," she said, extending her hand to him.

He shook her hand. "Our chance meeting two nights ago is still fresh in my memory."

"I took the liberty of sharing with my sister and her husband what took place that night," she said, taking a seat beside him at the table.

"I've been thinking a lot about it, too," he replied. "The burden you've been carrying alone for years has helped me. I thought I had a difficult time, but it pales in comparison to the trauma heaped upon you. I admire your courage and strength."

"Oh, you overestimate my handling of the situation, but I thank you for telling me. I, too, have experienced a renewal of hope. I really believe that I can face the future with a greater sense of commitment."

"My sister has pulled herself up from the ashes of despair, and we are very proud of her," Elaine said, embracing Kimberly.

"I have a request to make. Would you autograph my copy of one of your books?" Alvin asked, placing the book beside her. "A school teacher friend of mine is reading your book, *TEARS IN THE DARKNESS,* and called it your best book so far. I got a copy of that book from the library in Greenville and also read it. I agree, it's a tribute to the power of the human spirit."

Tears formed in Kimberly's eyes. "That book saved me from going mad. If you read it, then you've looked into my soul and saw a troubled woman on the edge."

"Our Kimberly has made us proud," George added. "The burden of grief losing Lee was bad enough, but her husband was one low-life son-of-a-bitch who cruelly tormented her as if she was an imbecilic slave. I never had a chance to lay my hands on him, and maybe it's a good thing. I would have broken his neck with pleasure. He robbed her of her self-respect and spent her money on booze and easy women."

"Now, now, George," Elaine calmly interrupted him. "Please help yourself, but before we eat, a silent prayer of thanksgiving is in order."

Alvin lowered his head and silently offered a heartfelt thanks for allowing him to become a friend to this close family. He was an only child deprived of the opportunity to share hardships and pleasures with siblings. He had close relations with nearby cousins, but that was not the same thing.

The meal progressed with ease and was filling. Most people are surprised at the amount of food a person can consume in the Maine forests. During the course of the meal he learned a lot more about Kimberly. She was a graduate of the University of Maine with a degree in history. Early history of the country was her specialty. Trials and tribulations of the past fascinated her. She had taught history at a high school for several years while she worked on her earlier historical novels. Ten years ago, she voluntarily quit teaching because she did not want her students to see that her world had been turned upside down.

Kimberly had also been a professional illustrator working for several publishers and magazine editorial staffs. That work sustained her when she gave up teaching. After she lost Lee, she lost all hope of putting her life together and was prepared to exit from the human race.

Alvin checked his watch. It was five o'clock. "I want to get back to Lily Bay before dark. Landing a float plane at night can be dangerous."

"We've been talking a lot about me long enough. Now you know me better than I know myself," Kimberly smiled. "What about you, Alvin? Your career in the Coast Guard must have been rewarding. I know that you commanded the patrol boat that responded to our fire on the yacht. The Coast Guard has a greater amount of goodwill with the population than any of the other services."

"The main thread that runs through the Coast Guard is the fact that they are at heart a life-saving organization. That function defines them. The Coast Guard works diligently to inspire its members. I wore the uniform with pride and miss the camaraderie that always existed on all of their vessels. Their response to emergencies are legendary as you have experienced, Kimberly. The hard fact to accept is that man cannot work miracles, and we are not able to save every victim. Human limitations of all types have got to be accepted without guilt. We have to rejoice for those who are saved and mourn those we could not. I know that now. I always knew it when I was responding to calls for help, but your daughter Lee was one failure that troubled me beyond reason..."

Chapter Eleven

Alvin watched Kimberly respond to his comment about not being responsible for those people who could not be saved by the Coast Guard.

She had listened carefully and shook her head in agreement. "Alvin, no one blames you or anyone else for Lee's death. It was a tragic act of fate. I never blamed myself. Her loss was so difficult because she left me in a world I was unprepared to face alone. Last night I took a good look at myself. Much of my problem has been selfishness. I was concerned about how events affected me. It's time I stopped and reached out to help others instead of taking. I've been taking from my sister and George who have been heroic in their support and compassion."

Elaine listened to her sister and said, "George and I have been waiting a long time for you to arrive at this point. Helping others in need is a fine way to also help ourselves. I've never been more proud of you, Kim, than I am right now. Compassion has always been one of your strengths. You were never selfish, and families look after family members."

"My sister has continued to grow," George reached across the table to take her hand in his. "Even when you were suffering from depression and alcoholism, there was never a trace of bitterness or hatred. Any criticism that you harbored you aimed at yourself. You never blamed anyone else for your problems. Even your husband, who must share a large percentage of the responsibility for your difficulties, got off easily. I don't hide my dislike of him. He was a very weak man who survived and lived off your strength and success. He was a true parasite."

Alvin had the feeling that he had attended a family reunion when the family had just received good news. Kimberly's decision to reach out to others in a more positive manner began to show. The deep lines about her mouth and eyes were eased, and she smiled more often.

She mentioned that she was going to attend more Alcoholic Anonymous meetings. The hospital where she spent several months was always looking for volunteers to help with the patients. Kim excused herself to get something in her room. She returned with a large sketch pad filled with several scenes visible from the deck on the log cabin looking west into some very beautiful sunsets.

"These are simple pencil sketches that I wanted to get down on paper so as to complete them at a later date after we've left. I'm anxious to start painting and doing illustrations again. The solitude and peace that exists here in the wilderness has helped me do some much needed self-examination."

She showed an enthusiasm for her work that brought out her love of nature. Alvin thought she had made a miraculous conversion from the withdrawn woman she was on the trip to Square Lake. She was making progress, and it ignited her creative instincts. That pleased her and those who loved her. From that moment Alvin was a supporter of the gifted lady who had defied all odds and rose from the depths of depravity.

Alvin left Square Lake feeling good about the events of the past few days. He had made new friends. For two weeks he carried food supplies up to the cabin. With each successive trip, he found Kimberly more motivated and involved in painting and sketches to be painted. The last time he dropped off food and milk, Kimberly was standing on the landing painting a canvas on her easel. She told him she liked doing pastoral scenes. She was wearing a large brimmed straw hat to shade the sun from her eyes.

He asked her for permission to see what she was doing. She was anxious to have his opinion. He saw that she was doing the scene before her with the lake in the foreground and Hedgehog Mountain in the background to the southwest and Mount McLean to the northwest, towering above the water. She colored the mountains in the background with a purple haze, highlighting their peaks with an orange tinge from the setting sun. It was a beautiful scene, igniting a certain amount of melancholy that sunsets often convey. It was the last moments of a day closing in a shroud of color.

"Kimberly, it's beautiful. I really like it. If I did not think so, I'd tell you so."

She was pleased with his response. "Everyone views a scene differently."

Alvin placed his cargo on the landing and made one trip to the cabin with arms loaded to capacity. George met him at the door. "I was being lazy, taking a nap, and did not hear your plane. I'll help you with the rest of the stuff. This will be your last trip with the supplies. I hate to see this vacation end."

"I'm glad you selected me to service your vacation, George. I like to think it was fate. Kimberly is a gifted artist. I checked the scene she's working on, and it's really nice."

"Elaine and I knew that it was just a question of time before she came out of her shell. She has a strong constitution. The name on your plane acted as a catalyst that brought all of the frustrations to the fore. She's ready to take on the real world now. We won't worry about her anymore."

"That's good news. She's a creative person. I've read her historical novels, and they are factually correct. I'm a little of a history buff," Alvin exclaimed. "I've got to get going, George. I'll see you back here in two days, weather permitting. If we have bad weather, it'll be the next day."

"Thanks, Alvin. It's been a pleasure," George said, carrying the last of the supplies into the cabin.

Alvin said good-bye to Kimberly. "I'll see you in a few days. I'm in a hurry today to see a couple of kids who have graciously allowed me to be a part of their lives. I promised to join them for a barbeque cookout in Alton."

"Enjoy yourself, Alvin. I think I'll put your plane in the scene. I love your title *GOLDEN ANGEL*. Thanks for everything. Good luck at the barbecue."

"Thanks, Kimberly. I like your hat," he smiled.

She turned to smile at him. "I thought you might. Until next time, Alvin."

"Until next time, Kimberly."

He lifted off the water and circled the landing, wiggling his wings in salute to her. She removed her straw hat and waved it at him. He liked having her for a friend.

Later in the day, Alvin drove his Studebaker truck into Merci's yard. Merle's Buick sedan was parked beside her Studebaker. He parked the truck, and before he could get out of the door, Jodi and Melody greeted him. He kneeled to embrace both of them. "It's nice to see you two again. I wanted to get down sooner, but I've been really busy flying. Business has been good."

"Grandmother told us you were busy and that you'd come when you could," Jodi said. "I've been sleeping out almost every night. There's a big horned owl that keeps me awake some nights with his calls from the tree beside the barn."

Alvin laughed. "The nights are owned by the nocturnal creatures, Jodi."

Melody wrapped her arms around his neck. "I've been practicing a lot on the violin. I can move my fingers better than when I first started."

"Will you play something for me before I leave, Melody?"

"Yes, that's why I've been practicing." She released her grip on his neck.

"Grandmother is in the kitchen, and Merle is in the barn. She doesn't like to have people looking over her shoulder," Jodi explained.

Alvin grabbed their two hands and walked towards the barn with them. "We'll keep Merle company while Grandmother does what she needs to do in the kitchen."

Merle met them at the screen door, opening it for them. "Hi, Merle. Jodi says his grandmother likes to be left alone in the kitchen, so we'll visit with you for a while. I have something I want to discuss with you."

"Merci does have a mind of her own," Merle replied and sat down in one of the Adirondack chairs.

Alvin took one beside him and told Merle that he met Kimberly Lambert on their fishing expedition. He did not divulge any of her private life, asking Merle for his opinion on her books if he had read any of them. "She's a University of Maine graduate, and I thought you and Merci may know her."

Merle replied that he did know her and was not impressed with her work.

"I'm surprised, Merle," Alvin exclaimed. "Her two historical novels and the latest one are all bestsellers. The people have purchased her work in large numbers. I would think that fact constitutes a certain amount of success. Do you agree?"

Merle was not comfortable. "Success in the marketplace does not make a writer a good one."

"Tell me, Merle, what does a good writer have that a bad writer does not have? Is it social prominence, money, or acceptable pedigree that makes a difference?"

"This is neither the time nor the place to get into technicalities, Alvin."

"You're an English Professor, Merle. I've read her three books and found the historical novels to be factual and accurate."

Merle spoke about the way the native people were treated by the colonists. "The founding of the country was based on grossly unfair treatment of the native population," he declared.

"I agree with you, Merle," Alvin continued. "The strong always defeat the weak. Isn't that the history of mankind?"

"Not exactly," Merle protested. "Our forefathers had superior weapons they used against the primitive tribes."

"Sure, we were wrong in displacing them the way we did. It's my understanding that the smaller native tribes along the Atlantic coast were cruelly overrun by the Delaware, Abenaki, Mohegan, Mohican and other more powerful tribes. Genocide was practiced on their own people, like the Pequots, simply because they were weaker. Their own kind were more ruthless than the British or the French in eliminating weaker communities. The strong always defeat the weak. One exception to that law of human society is a relatively recent phenomenon. Can you tell me about that exception, Professor?"

Merle was getting irritated by Alvin's forceful defense of his position. "At the moment, I can't think of one."

"Well, in this century, the Germans, Italians, Japanese and the Russians have all exerted their strength over weaker neighbors and certain elements within their population. All except the Russians have been defeated on the field of battle. The United States was stronger and successfully subdued them, yet we did not take the land away from them for our own use. Instead we rebuilt their homelands. The United States is one country that did not take land from the weak. That makes this nation an exception on the world stage. How do you explain that fact?"

"The United States exerted its imperialistic ways against many smaller communities," Merle stated.

"The Philippines were given their independence after the war. Hawaii and Puerto Rico are states that govern themselves today. I do not claim to be an authority," Alvin admitted.

"To continue this conversation is fruitless, Alvin. You have your opinions, and I have mine. In this free country that is our right, correct?"

"You're correct, Merle. Freedom is never free. It comes at a price that is very high to many families like Merci's, mine and thousands of others," Alvin replied, and walked away to look at the tent Jodi had set up beside the barn.

He climbed inside and sat down in the tent with Jodi. "I sleep sometimes with a friend out here. My first night alone was a little scary. Now I like it a lot. In the evening when it's a little cooler, I can watch the stars and pick out the North Star. Melody and grandmother slept out with me one night."

"That's nice, Jodi. I'm glad you're enjoying the tent."

"Mr. Stanchfield has started the charcoal, and Melody has gone in to help Grandmother carry out the food. You got Merle angry didn't you, Uncle Al?"

"I didn't mean to do that. After all, I'm an invited guest. I left the barn because I did not want to anger him anymore. We just don't agree on some things, that's all. I hope I was not rude."

"Grandmother disagrees with him quite a bit. I don't think he likes us around when he comes to see her. He doesn't like children. He's always after Melody to get him things like a glass of water or a bottle of ginger ale. She's a little afraid of him."

"I understand, Jodi," he said, slapping him on the back. "I see your grandmother and Melody coming out of the house to the barn. Let's go to meet them."

Merci smiled at him. "I saw your truck pull into the yard. A bright red truck stands out. I was in the middle of a mess in the kitchen," she said.

Alvin took the heavy tray of food from her. Merle opened the door for them. She looked at the grill and said, "Thanks for getting it going, Merle."

"I'd be glad to handle the grilling of the hot dogs and hamburgers. I left my chef's hat at home, but Jodi and I can get the job done," Alvin volunteered.

"I was going to ask you two for some help. You just volunteered," she sat beside Merle, and Melody took a seat beside her.

Alvin and Jodi filled the grill to capacity with hot dogs and hamburgers and closed the cover. Al turned to Merci. "I was talking with Merle here about a person I met way up near the Canadian border. She was part of a fishing expedition. Her name is Kimberly Lambert. I've read the three books she's written. Do you know her?"

"Yes, I remember Kimberly. I helped her locate some documents when she was researching the first two novels. She's a wonderful person. I was saddened by her decline. I've read her latest book and must say it's a magnificent study of a courageous woman. She was teetering on the edge at one time and returned triumphantly to take on the world. She's a dear soul who has suffered grievously."

Merci's opinion of Kimberly was different from Merle's. He sat stoically in silence, avoiding Alvin's searching glance. "I left there earlier today when she was on the landing painting a water scene." He wanted to share with Merci what took place between himself and Kimberly, but declined to do so with Merle present.

"Is she doing well, Alvin?" Merci asked.

"She seems at peace with herself up there in the wilderness. I understand she had a rough time with her husband."

"I never knew him. I'm glad she's survived the crisis in her life and come out swinging. It's what I would have expected of her. She's a strong person, and I'm glad to be her friend."

He reflected that Kimberly may also be fortunate to have Merci as a friend. The afternoon passed quickly. Merle excused himself soon after they finished eating. He courteously said good-bye to Alvin, wishing him success in his new business venture. He left without a word to the twins.

Merci and Alvin sat in the screened patio of the barn with a soft breeze blowing through the enclosure. They drank iced tea and watched Merle drive his Buick out of the driveway.

"Merle was quieter than usual," she mused.

Alvin did not want to tell her that he had been responsible for Merle's sour mood. "Everyone has their days," he said, passing it off with a flourish. "I see little Melody coming with her violin. She promised to play for me today." He opened the screen door for her. "I was hoping that you would not forget, Melody."

His enthusiasm pleased her as she placed the case on the picnic table and took out the violin. "I've been practicing a lot this summer," she told him. "Grandmother bought me a song book filled with a lot of the popular songs they play on the radio. I can play some of them. Some are pretty hard, and I have to practice the finger movements."

"She's doing just fine, Alvin. I'm so proud of her. She has a natural ear for tone and rhythm. Her music teacher is enthused with her progress. What selections are you going to play, Melody?" her grandmother asked.

She quietly listened to the tune of the strings and was satisfied. "I practiced this one for Uncle Al. I think it's the most beautiful song of all. It makes me sad, especially the ending," she exclaimed, placing the instrument to her chin.

Her short fingers moved easily over the strings. Alvin instantly recognized her selection, *Londonderry Aire*. Melody became a different person as soon as she started the composition. She closed her eyes and became a part of the music, concentrating on her playing. He, too, loved music and was surprised at how accomplished she had become in such a short time. Her timing was flawless as she progressed from note to note with a smooth departure and introduction of the individual notes. The transition was smooth and continuous and was the work of an artist. She ended the selection, holding the final notes as if they were fading into the distance. Merci looked at Alvin who was touched by the feelings Melody gave to the Irish folk song.

Melody ended and opened her eyes, looking into his for a reaction. He held his arms out to her. "You have succeeded beyond all of my expectations, dear Melody. I'm so proud of you. Your playing is beautiful. That's my favorite song, and I've never heard it played with as much heart and soul as you've just accomplished."

"It was beautiful, Melody," Merci added proudly.

Melody was pleased with the praise from the two people in the world she loved the most. "Would you like to hear one more that I've heard on the radio?"

"You bet, Melody. You and that violin have come together almost as one. You've made me very happy. It's so nice to hear good music. What are you going to do for an encore?"

"*Harbor Lights,*" she replied and began the piece. It was obvious that she liked playing the instrument. When she had finished, Alvin, her grandmother, and Jodi whistled and clapped their hands. Melody was beaming with their response. She gently placed the violin and bow in the case and turned to Alvin with eyes aglow. "I'm happy that you like my playing, Uncle Al."

Chapter Twelve

Jodi saw the mailman drive up to the mailbox while Melody was putting her violin away in the case. "May I get the mail, Grandmother?"

"That would be nice, Jodi. Thank you."

"You have these kids well-trained," Alvin grinned.

"They have enriched my life since I brought them to Maine," she replied.

Melody snapped her violin case closed and took it off the table holding it in her arms. "This violin is the best gift I could ever have. Thank you, Uncle Al. I love you."

"I love you too, Melody."

She smiled and skipped all the way to the house.

"That little girl has blossomed with confidence since she started lessons. I was concerned for her when we first came home. Her affection for you is sincere."

"That makes me proud," Alvin remarked, watching Melody. "She reminds me of that small child that belonged to Kimberly. I haven't told you about that incident," he continued, telling her about the tragic accident, her death, and the naming of his plane. He also shared his confrontation with Kimberly.

Merci was shocked. "What an amazing story, Alvin. I had read about her losing her daughter in an accident at sea. God works in strange ways."

"I did not share that with Merle. He seemed quite negative to Kimberly's writing. I liked it and asked him why. He really could not tell me." Alvin was relieved to bring up the subject with Merci.

Jodi placed the mail on the picnic table in front of his grandmother. She sorted through it and anxiously opened a letter. "This is a letter from the twin's mother, Celia Lane." She read it in silence and placed it on the table with the other mail.

86

"Is anything wrong, Merci?"

"She wants to take custody of the twins and take them back to Georgia," Merci explained, holding her anger. "As a mother she has that right, and I respect that fact. Neither of the twins want to return with her. Melody is just beginning to come out of the shell she had built around her. She was frightened, plain and simple. I'm going to fight it."

Seeing how emotional Merci became, Alvin supported her position. "I agree with you. They are adorable children that anyone could love. They're old enough and intelligent enough to make up their own mind. They seem to be happy and well adjusted here with you. I'll help you in any way I can."

"I appreciate that. The twins always look forward to your visits. This past year they've done well in school. What do I do if the mother insists on taking them to Georgia, and they do not want to go?" she asked helplessly.

"I'm sure the law is on the side of the mother. However, there's a point where their opinion has to be considered. Are you prepared to take her to court and have her declared unfit?"

"No, and I would not want to place the children in a position where they have to choose. Perhaps I should meet with Celia and see what develops. Maybe I'm prejudging her. I have a favor to ask, Alvin."

"You have but to ask, Merci."

"When Celia Lane visits us, would you be present to forge a decision that is acceptable for everyone?"

"I'd be glad to do that," he replied. "What about Merle? After all, you two are engaged to marry. He may not like it."

She thought for a few seconds before answering. "Ever since you met us on the road, you've been a part of the twins life. Merle views the children as a problem with few solutions. I have not been able to change his mind."

"Then it's settled. I'll do it for you and the twins. If Merle objects, he can go in the corner and sulk."

She laughed. "Sometimes he has a lot of growing up to do. He thinks the children belong to the mother. I would too if she was responsible. We'll decide that when she arrives in Maine."

"Do you know when she's coming?"

"Sometime next week," Merci replied.

"You call me when you know, and I'll be here. If I'm unavailable, please leave a message with my answering service.

This has been a pleasant visit, Merci. Thanks for inviting me. You have a lovely place here."

"It requires a lot of maintenance, but we manage."

He stood up and held out his hand to her. She embraced him and rested her head on his chest. "Thanks for being our friend, Chief." Then she kissed him.

He returned her kiss and held her in his arms. It was unexpected, yet it seemed natural. "I'll wait for your call. Do not worry, dear Lady. Things have a way of working out."

"Your support means a lot to me," she whispered, releasing him.

"I'll say 'so long' to the kids and head back to Lily Bay."

On his way home, Alvin thought about what took place between him and Merci. She was engaged to Merle, and he had to be careful. The soft spoken librarian would be easy to love. He could end up getting hurt. By the time he pulled into his driveway at Lily bay, he had dismissed the event, rationalizing that she was thankful for his support of the children. To go beyond that was dangerous territory.

His last trip to Square Lake took place in perfect flying weather, sunshine and low winds. By the time he tied up to the landing, George had carried all of the luggage from the cabin and placed it on the landing ready for easy loading.

"Good morning, George. It's a good day for a plane ride. I hope your stay has been a pleasant experience for you and your wife. I know that I'll remember it for a long time."

"Kimberly is returning from this fishing trip a different person than the one you dropped off two weeks ago. You've made a positive difference, Alvin. Both Elaine and I are thankful for that," George told him, handing the luggage for Alvin to pack in the storage compartment behind the passenger seats.

"I've been able to put to rest a lot of guilt that was beginning to be a heavy load. Kimberly has made a difference for me. I wish her well."

"Here come the ladies," George announced. "Sam will be along later."

Elaine and Kimberly were both dressed in light summer blouses with blue jeans. They walked to the landing side by side. Alvin noticed how they looked alike with similar hair style and green eyes. "Good morning, ladies," he greeted them.

88

Kimberly quietly acknowledged him with a nod and a smile. She turned to look across the water to the distant horizon and slowly looked back at the cabin, pausing a few seconds before accepting Alvin's hand to climb into the plane.

"Thanks, Alvin. I leave this place with some reluctance. It has been a wonderful experience for me. I thank you for contributing to the healing that has taken place in this wilderness."

"We've both grown from this experience, Kimberly. Secure your seat belts. I'll make a turn around the cabin so that you can see where you've been these past two weeks."

"That will be nice," Kimberly remarked, fastening her seat belt and adjusting her microphone. She was at peace with herself. Once they became airborne, he made the circle above the cabin. "I've loved the moving words of the dead Royal Air Force pilot, John Magee, who wrote: 'the long delirious burning blue; I've topped the wind-swept heights with easy grace; where never lark, or even eagle flew... and touched the face of God.' They have special meaning to those who fly. I've found inspiration in them also."

"Magee's words have special meaning to every person who feels a passion for flying. I plan to stop at Greenville for refueling. Then we'll fly directly for Winter Harbor. Would any of you like to have a late breakfast? It's just a few steps to one of the best restaurants in Greenville."

"That sounds nice," Elaine replied, grabbing her husband's arm. "A meal someone else has prepared will be welcome. George made the coffee every day, and I can say that it was always too strong."

George smiled at her. "Don't believe it, Alvin."

Kimberly too was amused. "George called my sister's coffee troubled water."

Alvin taxied to the gasoline service landing at Folsom's Airways and secured the plane. He pointed to the restaurant right across the bay. "You folks can go ahead to the restaurant. I'll service the plane and be along shortly."

While he was methodically making a pre-flight inspection of the plane, a familiar voice interrupted him. "Hello, stranger," Lois said. "I saw your plane land."

"Hi, Lois," he replied. "It's nice to see you. I've been meaning to stop by to see you, but business has been brisk. What are you doing in Greenville?"

"I came up to do some shopping and was hoping I'd catch you at Lily Bay. I saw your passengers leave the plane and walk to the restaurant."

"Yes, I plan to get a bite, too, after checking the plane. Why don't you join us? I'll buy you a breakfast."

"I'll let you," she answered, linking her arm in his.

"We'll join the folks I took on a fishing expedition at Square Lake. You'll like them."

The restaurant was filled with tourists and local residents. George was waving to him from a corner next to the water with a nice view of the bay. Alvin introduced Lois to the three strangers. Lois took a seat next to Kimberly.

"Alvin and I are old classmates. I walked to school with him every day since we were in the first grade." Lois recognized Kimberly Lambert's name. "I've read your latest book and found it a moving experience. Your writing comes from the heart. I envy people with that gift of creativity. What a pleasant surprise. I'm glad Alvin invited me to tag along. He's been a dear friend since childhood."

Alvin and Lois ordered poached eggs on toast and coffee. Lois meant what she had said about Kimberly's book and found it interesting to study the talented author with a modest air and unassuming attitude. The book had described a person that had been the object of self-destructive habits and a passion for life. Her calm and humble mannerisms were in direct contrast to the actual life she had experienced. She smiled at Alvin several times during the meal. Lois assumed, uncomfortably, that the two had become good friends.

George, Elaine, and Kimberly finished their meals and took advantage of the rest rooms. Alvin and Lois walked alone to the plane. "Have you given any more thought to the teaching job in Wells?" he asked.

"Would it make any difference to you, Alvin?"

"I would not ask if I wasn't interested, Lois."

"I wanted to spend some time with you, but I see you're busy. I'll catch you later."

"I'll be back in a few hours. I could see you then."

"Would you be disappointed if I did not wait around?"

"Come now. What's wrong, Lois?"

"I could ask you the same thing, Alvin. Lately you're distant and preoccupied. The Al I remembered is not around anymore, and I miss him. That's all."

He placed an arm around her waist and said: "I have been busy, Lois, more so than I expected. I haven't been intentionally avoiding you. If I hurt you, I'm sorry. My old friend should be able to understand that and celebrate with me."

She laid her head against his shoulder. "I'll wait for you at your place in Lily Bay. Be careful up there, Alvin. I do worry about you."

"You know where the key is; make yourself at home. I'll be back by nightfall, and I'll be careful," he answered, releasing her to double-check the condition of the floats.

George and Elaine said good-bye to Lois and took their positions in the plane. Kimberly held back to be alone with Lois. "I appreciate your kind words for my book. Do not be afraid. I am not competing with you for Alvin's affection. He's a dear friend that I will always hold close to my heart. I believe he feels the same way. I'm not a threat to you. It has been nice visiting with you. Good-bye, Lois."

"Good-bye, Kimberly, bon voyage."

Alvin started the plane after everyone had fastened their seat belts. He waved to Lois and started his run to the west for a liftoff. The flight to the coast was uneventful. He reconnoitered the landing area at Winter Harbor and circled it several times, waiting for small boats to vacate the area. Once it was clear, he went in fast and taxied to the landing. He jumped on the landing with a mooring line and wrapped it around a post.

"Well, folks, this is the end of the line for us. I'll pile your luggage on the dock for you. It's been a pleasure, Elaine and George."

A stranger to Alvin had been standing near the landing watching the passengers step out of the plane. Kimberly recognized the man and approached him. George told him that it was Kimberly's publisher, John Lisbon. The conversation between the two soon became heated when Kimberly slapped him on the face and screamed, "John, I'm not going to accept any such proposal from you. That part of my life is over. I'm fully capable of making decisions by myself. You don't own me. Get out of here and leave me alone."

George dropped a suitcase and started towards John Lisbon who left in a staccato of foul language aimed at Kimberly.

"It's hard to believe that the man is a gifted editor," Kimberly declared out of breath. "I can't believe I've finally called it quits with him. He's a control freak who led me around like a puppy dog." She turned to Alvin fastening the cargo door on the plane. "The fishing expedition, with you as our faithful guide, has made me strong enough to do what should have been done a long time ago."

Alvin grinned, "He left in a hurry, that's for sure. I'm happy for you, Kimberly. This parting makes me sad. I'll never forget you."

"Thank you for being the kind person you are, Alvin. You gave a wonderful tribute to my precious Lee's memory. I'll never forget that. Would it be presumptuous of me to suggest that instead of good-bye we say so long? Friends are a rare gift, and I don't want to lose you...." She kissed him and walked off the landing.

Chapter Thirteen

Alvin was processing firewood in preparation for the harsh winters that were the norm for the region. He had purchased a new McCulloch chainsaw to make the work more efficient. Two days after he had dropped off Kimberly at Winter Harbor, he had received a frantic phone call from Merci telling him that Celia Lane was on her way to Maine to get the children. She had made an appointment to meet in two days. Alvin told her that he was free and would be there when the mother arrived.

The second call from Merci came while he was unloading the truck piling firewood in the attached shed behind the cabin. She told him the time of Celia's arrival. "I'll be there early, Merci. Don't get all worked up about it."

He arrived an hour before Celia was scheduled to meet Merci and the twins. His first act was to sit down with the twins to discuss what was about to take place. He asked them bluntly what they wanted to do and why did they not want to go with their mother.

Jodi was quick to answer his questions. "Our mother can be very kind and fun to be with sometimes, and she was often demanding that we be quiet and not bother the boyfriends she was entertaining. Some of the soldiers were good to us, others ignored us. When Mother started to drink whiskey the men brought with them, she got angry easy and hit us a lot if we bothered her."

Alvin listened without comment. "What about you, Melody? Did you feel the same way as Jodi? Don't be afraid to tell your grandmother and me what you really think. That's important for us to know."

"I'm not afraid," she replied.

Alvin kneeled in front of her and took her two hands in his. "The truth is important, Melody. If you would rather be with

93

your mother, then it's okay to say so. Your grandmother and I both want you and Jodi to be happy, and we love you very much. Your mother also loves you because she's your mother."

"When Jodi and I were with mother, I was scared when her friends talked loud and angry after we went to bed. Jodi was slapped more than I was, but there was one soldier that was very kind, and he told mother to take better care of us. We never saw him again. I want to stay with Grandmother, and so does Jodi."

He hugged her and said, "No child should ever be afraid of a parent. Now when your mother comes, be nice to her and answer her questions honestly. Maybe you could play your violin for her."

That drew a quick reply from Melody. "Mother was always out of money, and she sold a lot of things in the house to get money for food. If I showed her the violin, she might sell it to get money. I don't want her to see the beautiful instrument you gave to me."

Alvin looked at Merci. They both shook their heads in dismay. Merci told her, "Don't worry about that, Melody. Your Uncle Al and I understand, and we'll do the best we can. Of course, when you're eighteen, you two can independently chose where you want to live. That's a long ways off. If your mother decides to take this to court, we may lose, and there is nothing we can do about it. We have no legal right to keep you."

"That's not fair, Grandmother," Jodi challenged her statement.

"No, Jodi, it isn't fair," Alvin replied. "However, it's the law. If it comes to that, you and Melody will have a chance to tell a judge in private how you feel. Then he will make a decision based on the truth you've told him."

"I see a car coming up the driveway," Melody announced.

Alvin saw a 1950 Pontiac coupe with a man driving it. He got out of the car and checked out the land around the house and barn. He then opened the door for Celia Lane to get out of the car. Merci opened the door to greet them. "Welcome to Maine, Celia. You'll find it cooler than Georgia."

Celia was taller than Merci and a little heavier. She was dressed in a light blue blouse and a pair of dark blue slacks, wearing her dark hair full about her shoulders. She was apprehensive with a slight scowl on her face. Merci held out her hand to greet the woman her son had married. At one time, she thought her son had made a good choice. "It's nice to see you again. The twins are in the house. Won't you please come inside where we can visit for a while?"

"This is an important trip for me, Merci. This is Jack Hayes. He's a sergeant in the Marine Corps. We're engaged to marry," Celia stated firmly.

"I'm glad to meet you, Sergeant Hayes. I'm Merci Lane, the twins' grandmother. Please come inside," she said, pointing to the front entrance of her New England style home.

The twins were anxiously sitting on a couch in the sitting room with Alvin. When they saw their mother enter the room, they jumped up and ran to her. Celia was touched by their enthusiasm. Merci introduced Alvin to Celia and Sergeant Hayes. The two men sized up one another and shook hands. Hayes was a short, heavily built man with a pugnacious air of superiority. His stance discouraged familiarity.

"May I get either of you some refreshments, coffee or ice tea?" Merci suggested, hoping that the conversation would be reasonable.

"No thanks," Hayes answered for Celia.

"I want to start this visit off with an offer for you, Celia. Why don't you take the twins for a day or so to visit and enjoy each other's company? They need to spend time with their mother and I wouldn't be surprised if their mother needed them even more. It's important for you to know that I am not your enemy, Celia."

Hayes answered for her. "It would be crowded in a hotel room for an all night stay."

"Well," Merci looked directly at Celia. "Why don't you tell me what you want, Celia? You're the mother."

"I could never give them a home such you have, Merci. I remember Robert talking about this house and what it was like in Maine. The children look happy here."

"School will be starting soon. They're doing well. I've sent you copies of their report cards," Merci said.

"Yes, they got good grades in Georgia, too. Jack and I came to Maine to bring them back with us. I have the right to do that." Celia gave Merci a defiant look as if to test her.

Merci decided that neither of them were in any mood to be civil or to negotiate in good faith. Therefore, she framed their conversation with hard questions. "Yes, that's true, Celia. How do you plan to support them? Do you want them because you love them or because they add to the amount of welfare payment you receive? Are you working at a steady job? I do not ask these personal questions to be unkind. I'm simply concerned about the twins' welfare."

The questions cut through the indecision and got to the heart of the problem. They got a quick response from Hayes. "Those questions are none of your business. She's their mother and can do what she wants with them."

"Except for one important problem, Sergeant Hayes," Alvin stated with a calm voice. "The children have rights, too, and that's the only reason I'm here. What if Melody and Jodi do not want to go with you, Celia?"

"Who is this man?" Celia asked, beginning to lose her composure.

"I'm a friend to the twins and their grandmother. Merci's questions are pertinent to the situation. They should not be difficult to answer. The twins deserve better than welfare payments to live on."

"Not everyone can be a college employee like Merci," Celia stated sarcastically. "I want to leave soon and take the children with me."

Merci calmly announced, "I can't allow that, Celia."

"She's their mother, lady. Don't you get it?" Hayes threateningly raised his voice.

"Watch your tone, Hayes. You're not impressing anyone, and the kids are frightened. I think it would be best for the twins to be sent to their rooms. They don't need to hear this," Alvin suggested, looking at Merci.

She nodded and sent them upstairs to their rooms. Melody looked at her mother and then to Jack. Alvin saw fear in her eyes, and went to her, kneeling to hold her in his arms. "Things will work out, Melody, don't worry. Go up with Jodi. Your grandmother has to settle this disagreement." She hugged him and ran upstairs.

Alvin then turned to confront Jack and Celia. "I'm a friend, and that is the first time I've seen fear in Melody's eyes. She's too small and fragile to be afraid of her blood family. I am probably speaking out of line, and I apologize if I offend anyone by what I want to say. You are their mother, Celia, but you've

96

abdicated that privilege by your destructive habits with drugs and alcohol. You created a level of fear and apprehension that no child should have to experience. If you want the twins to return to North Carolina with you, you've got to have a court order to do so. I'm sure that Merci will petition the court for them to remain where they are for their mental and physical welfare. Do you really want to subject your loved ones to that kind of trauma?"

"How does that change the fact that I'm their mother?" Celia cried.

"Prove to us that you have the means to support them, Celia," Merci explained in a calm voice. "When I took them over a year ago, you were in a drunken stupor that scared the twins. Right now, I smell booze on you and Hayes. Would they even be safe traveling with you?"

Hayes snapped back at her. "Lady, you have a talent for insulting people with your know-it-all attitude. We don't have to have your approval to take the twins."

Celia began to cry and Hayes directed her to the door.

"I'm sorry to have things end this way, Celia," Merci followed after them with tears running down her cheeks. "You must know that Robert would approve of the children being with me. I never meant to keep them from you, but your destructive lifestyle left me with no other option. Please, try to pull your life together so that Jodi and Melody can be proud of their mother."

Celia and Sergeant Hayes left the house in a hurry. The twins had been watching from an upstairs window and ran down to see what had happened. The meeting had not gone well, and Merci met them in a frustrated state of mind.

"Will mother be coming back?" Jodi asked.

"I don't believe so, Jodi. By the way, have you ever seen your mother with Sergeant Hayes?"

"No," Melody replied quickly. "I don't like him."

Alvin smiled to himself. A child's intuition agreed with his private instincts.

Merci sat down on the couch with a worried look. "I wish things had gone better. My son married the woman and he must have seen more to her than she's projecting right now. It's a sad day, and nothing was accomplished."

"Don't expect miracles, Merci, until she changes her lifestyle. Her friend, Hayes, was not what I'd call an outstanding member of the human race. He's dominating her right now, and that doesn't bode well for a happy future."

"Thanks for helping out, Chief. You made a difference, and I appreciate the support."

"I've got an idea," Alvin announced, looking at Merci. "What do you say if we all go out to have a lunch and go to a movie? There's a great one showing that I saw advertised: *The Diary of Anne Frank.* The twins should enjoy it."

"That sounds like a good idea," Merci said. "What do you twins think?"

"Oh, yeh, that would be fun," Jodi responded.

"I think so, too," Melody smiled.

"Then it's settled. The twins can ride in the back of the truck where I've placed some comfortable seats next to the cabin. Let's mount up." Alvin was pleased that his suggestion was received so well.

Later that evening, Alvin was on his way back to Lily Bay, mulling over the events of the day. After the movie they had eaten at a good restaurant in Bangor. It was a happy outing that overshadowed the visit with the twins' mother. He thought how sad it was that a mother could so completely alienate her children. The twins deserved better than she was able to give them. They were fortunate that Merci had the courage to remove them from a poisonous environment.

The movie, *The Diary of Anne Frank,* was a sobering experience for all who saw it. Merci was especially touched by it and was quieter than usual for the rest of the evening. Alvin headed back shortly after dropping Merci and the twins off. He had a heavy schedule the next day, resupplying two fishing expeditions he had inserted in the northern wilderness.

The road between Bangor and Monson was lightly traveled, and he was making good time. He always had a warm feeling whenever he entered the Town of Monson. His roots were there, and his childhood had been filled with warm memories. He thought of Lois and the last time they were together. She had waited at his cabin when he returned from Winter Harbor. She was standing on the landing and helped him secure the Beaver to the dock.

"I'm glad you waited for me," he said, embracing her. They had been important friends ever since they were small children, and they probably knew each other even better than they knew themselves.

"I have some boulla rolls Mother made this morning, and the percolator is ready to be turned on."

"It's nice to come home. You looked a little worried when I left this afternoon. I felt bad for that."

She laid her head against his shoulder as they walked into the cabin. "I apologize for letting my jealousy show. It was childish, and I'm sorry. I wanted to make amends."

He smiled at her impulsive nature and her inherent decency and sense of fair play. He always suspected that those virtues were what made her an excellent teacher in the classroom. That evening she had told him that she was taking the job at Wells for one year as a trial run. It was a little more money, and her mother would join her for an extended stay at the seacoast. She promised to return whenever she could to see him and check on the house. It was about a four hour trip from Wells.

It was not too late to stop at her mother's place for a short visit. The lights were on, and Lois's Rambler was parked in the driveway. He stopped and knocked on the door. A disheveled Lois ran to open the door.

"Thank God it's you, Alvin. Mother just fell down the stairs…"

Chapter Fourteen

Lois grabbed his arm and pulled him into the hallway where her mother was lying on the floor at the foot of the stairs. Alvin immediately checked for a pulse. It was a rapid one, and he looked at her pupils for signs of a concussion. The eyes seemed normal. That was a good sign! He was a certified EMT (emergency medical technician) all during his career in the Coast Guard. He ran his hands over arms and legs, feeling for any signs of broken bones. Her heartbeat was still rapid, but that would be normal for the frightened woman who had fallen down the stairs.

"Lois, help me turn your mother over on her stomach. I want to check for a possible broken back. She has a bruise that's turning bluish red on her left side which might have broken a rib or two. Let's check her back. Easy now..."

Lois gently placed a pillow under her mother's head and helped Alvin keep her body straight and aligned properly. "I don't see any evidence of a compound fracture anywhere on her body. How far up the stairs was she when she fell, Lois?"

"I didn't see her, but I heard her roll off some of the steps."

"I have a first aid kit in my truck glove box. Would you get it for me, Lois?"

She ran outside and returned with the large first aid kit. Alvin said, "I want to revive her with smelling salts."

He grabbed a vial and broke it, passing it beneath her mother's nose. She tried to turn away from it, but Alvin kept it beneath her nostrils until she opened her eyes and pushed the salts away with her right hand. Another good sign!

"You fell down the stairs, Mom. Where do you hurt?" Lois asked, thankful for her alertness.

"I hurt on my side, and it hurts to breathe."

100

"I think you may have a broken rib or two, Mrs. Carson. We should take you to the Greenville Hospital for an x-ray to be sure. Do you hurt anywhere else?" Alvin asked calmly.

"Do I really have to go to the hospital?"

Lois was quick to answer, "Yes, we're taking you. Alvin is correct in suggesting it. I'll get the car ready for you."

Alvin carried Mrs. Carson to the Rambler and gently deposited her in the passenger seat which could be reclined for comfort. "You really need to be checked by a doctor. I'll be following you to Greenville," he informed her.

"Thank you, Alvin. You have a gentle touch much like your father. I hate to be a bother," Mrs. Carson complained.

"Since when is a dear friend ever a bother, Mrs. Carson? I'm glad I stopped by to see Lois."

"And I'm relieved that you did, too," Lois said, placing a sweater around her mother's shoulders.

Mrs. Carson remained alert all the way to the hospital. They used the emergency room entrance and helped the attendants get her on the wheeled stretcher. She waved to Lois and Alvin as she was being pushed into the examination room.

"Let's grab a cup of coffee, Lois. This could be a long wait," he suggested, guiding her to a small waiting room with a self-serve coffee station.

Lois was exhausted and collapsed into a chair. "This is the first time I've ever seen my mother injured or seriously sick. Most of the time, she's full of energy."

"Would you like a coffee?"

"Yes, thanks, Alvin"

He poured her a cup and remembered that she took one sugar and a dab of cream. As he handed it to her, he grinned. "Do you have a boulla roll in your purse?"

She smiled and took the coffee.

"Your mom is in good hands. She'll be just fine, Lois. She was lucky. She could have been seriously hurt. I bet they'll want to keep her for a couple of days for observation."

Lois sipped her coffee. "Mm, that tastes good."

"Once we hear from the doctor, she'll probably be sedated. We could leave your Rambler here, and you could come to Lily Bay with me for a good night's rest. You look tired, Lois. I have a fire patrol first thing in the morning and can bring you to Greenville."

She looked at him with weary eyes. "Your offer sounds good. What a fool Meredith was to cheat on you. God punished her for that."

He didn't answer; he simply took a chair beside her and placed a comforting hand on her arm. She never loved him as much as she did in that silent moment in the hospital waiting room. He saw what was in her heart. They both had the knack of being able to read each others minds' and to finish their sentences. That joint familiarity was part of the bond that cemented their relationship. He was proud to call her a friend. Her deep sense of values was what defined her as a person and an inspiring teacher in the classroom.

An hour later, a doctor came into the waiting room to announce that her mother was going to be fine. "She has a broken rib which will heal in time without any problem. She also has numerous bruises over her body but nothing serious."

"How long will she have to stay in the hospital, Doctor?" Lois asked anxiously.

"I'd like to have her stay for a couple of days. You'll be able to talk to her in the morning. She's resting well right now. She's in good health and will come out of this scare as good as new, but she'll have to be careful about radical body movements. Moderate exercise is good for her."

"Thank you, Doctor. Leave word with her nurse that I'll see her first thing in the morning."

Alvin rose to shake his hand, also. "Thanks, Doctor. Lois will rest better now knowing that her mom is in good hands."

Lois locked her Rambler and got into Alvin's truck. He held the door open for her. She was quiet on the way to Lily Bay. The moon was full and reflected on the glistening waves of the lake. She was tired and was glad to accept his offer to stay at his place. He turned into the driveway and came to a stop with the moon shining directly into the truck, making it as light as day.

"You have a beautiful place here, Alvin. I'm glad for you. You deserve it," she said, getting out of the truck. "Your red Studebaker goes over the road very nicely."

"I really like it. I'd be lost without a truck up here."

He unlocked the front door, showing her where the key is hidden under a screen for the kitchen window. He pointed to the guest room and to the bathroom. "If you'd like a pair of my pajamas, I'll get them for you. They may be a little large, but..." he laughed.

"Thanks, Alvin. "I'll take the pajamas. I'm exhausted. A good night's sleep will be welcome."

"I'll fix breakfast for us in the morning and take you to Greenville with the plane. Then I'll start my fire patrol to the north. It's nice having you for a guest, Lois."

She wrapped her arms around him and held him in a tight embrace. "My friend is the same person I've known so well over the years. Again, thanks for being you." She kissed him and went into the bathroom.

He retired, too. It had been a most eventful day. "Rest well, Lois. I'll get you up in the morning."

"Goodnight, Alvin."

That night, a full moon filled the cabin with light. The days were getting shorter, and the harvest moon shone brighter than ever. Across the bay loons called to each other in their distinctive melancholic voices that evoked thoughts of medieval times. The calls of the loons were matched by the gentle whirr of the wind flowing through the white pine tree canopies that surrounded the cabin.

Lois was lulled to sleep by the soft whirr of the wind blowing through the trees. She was content; she was with her Alvin...

Alvin also remained awake listening to the loons and wind and thinking about what had taken place with the twins' mother and about their grandmother. The gentle lady was engaged to Merle, but for a long time, Alvin had to fight emotions that often stirred within him. He had a feeling that they were reciprocated and over and over he asked the question – was it the twins or their grandmother which was the greater attraction? He was having a hard time to answer the question honestly.

At the same time, there was the ever faithful and caring Lois. She would always be a dear friend. Their long childhood held too many warm memories for it to be a simple friendship. He was always concerned for her happiness and welfare. He expected that she was more attracted to him than he was ready to declare for her, and that made their relationship awkward at times. He respected her for many reasons, but most of all for her simple honesty and consistency. Smart and socially active, she

103

had many admirers, but she chose to remain alone after Carl's death. He admired her for that kind of loyalty. Sleep eventually came to him with no resolutions in sight.

Alvin was up at the break of day, turning on the pot of coffee, and taking a quick shower which probably woke Lois. When he stepped out of the bathroom, she was waiting to get in.

"The coffee is about ready, Lois. How about a poached egg on toast?"

"That would be nice, Alvin," she replied.

"That's my specialty."

They sat down to eat breakfast together and reviewed what was ahead of them. "What are your plans for the day, Alvin?"

"I have a lot of traveling to do today. First, I'll do a fire patrol flight to the Canadian border, then on to Lac St. Jean in Quebec with a supply of food for one of my fishing expeditions. On my return I'll do another fire patrol back to Moosehead."

"You have an active day ahead of you, and I know you're anxious to get going. You do a good cup of coffee. I'll tell Mother you'll be busy and may not be in until tomorrow."

He replied, cleaning off the table, "I'll do my best. I expect she'll be impatient to be home. I've got to call my supplier to make sure the load is ready."

While he was doing that, Lois cleaned off the counter and rinsed the dishes. As they were walking to the plane, he joked with her. "Were my pajamas a little long for you last night?"

"Just a tad," she laughed, climbing into the passenger seat of the plane.

"It's going to be a good day for flying," he remarked, starting the plane. He checked his instrument panel to see that all systems were working and slowly idled away from the dock. "Relax, Lois. It'll be a little rough until we get airborne."

The moment of liftoff, he rammed the throttle to full power. Lily Bay was only a few miles from Folsom's Airways in Greenville Village. He circled the area to be sure there were no boats in the busy water channel of the cove. He gently touched down and idled to the dock. His supply of canned goods were already stacked on the dock he used to refuel.

"Give my best to your mother. I'll see you when I return," he said.

"Is that a promise?"

"Sure, weather permitting. Pilots are a slave to the changes to the weather. It was nice having you for a short visit."

"Thanks for the hospitality, Alvin. You be careful out there. You're heading into pretty wild country after you cross the Saint Lawrence River. I worry about you." She kissed him, looking at the pile of boxes. "Do you want me to help you with those?"

"Thanks just the same. I can handle it, Lois."

She walked around the cove to the village, waving before she was out of sight. He returned her wave and finished securing the load in the cargo area of the plane. Then he topped up the fuel tank and did a thorough preflight inspection prior to his long flight into the Canadian wilderness. He had enough fuel to get to Lac St. Jean.

Alvin carried out his normal fire patrol procedures and called in when he crossed the border into Canada. At that point he called Canadian Air Control to inform them of his flight to Lac St. Jean and return the same day. He also gave them his "Golden Angel" call signal. He had crossed the Saint Lawrence River near Montimagny where he picked up a strong radio signal that would direct him to the mouth of the Mistassini River where it empties into Lac St. Jean. That was the location of a small float plane service center.

He received clearance to land on the lake slightly north of the river's mouth where he saw a large commercial dock. He had come 230 miles in less than two hours. The waters on Lac St. Jean were much more turbulent with larger waves than on Moosehead Lake. He landed so as to be close to the dock to cut down his travel in open water where it was easy to capsize a float plane. A small truck was backed out to the dock to receive his load. He told the service attendant to refuel the plane while he unloaded the cargo.

Once the plane was empty, he went into the service center for a cup of coffee and a ham sandwich. He also got an update on weather conditions. He had already registered his return flight over the same route. While he was eating his sandwich, a radio dispatcher approached him with an emergency "mayday" signal from Lake Albanel.

"Sir, I've just received this message from the small native village on the lake. They have a young man who was seriously injured in a fall onto some rocks. He needs surgery immediately. There are no planes available in the area except yours. Could you make the flight? It's about 160 miles north of Lac St. Jean."

"You're sure there aren't any military planes available?"

"No float planes, Sir."

"I'll take it," Alvin replied, rushing to his plane. "As soon as I'm airborne, vector me the correct bearing to the village in question and alert the village that I'm on my way. I don't speak French."

"It won't matter, Sir. I'll be with you going and coming. Good luck, Sir."

Alvin started the plane and buckled up, pushing the throttle to full speed. The water on the lake was rough, and he did not want to take a chance on being pulled under, so he kept the plane in a straight line during takeoff.

"Lac St. Jean Dispatch, this is *Golden Angel*. I am airborne on a course of ten degrees west of north. I have a weak radio signal and will follow it."

"*Golden Angel*, you are now following the beacon from the village at Lake Albanel. It will get stronger as you get nearer to the village. Good luck and Godspeed!"

Chapter Fifteen

The dispatcher was correct; the signal got stronger and louder by the mile. He had never flown this far into the Canadian northland with his plane. He estimated about an hour to reach the native village. The landscape below was a vast unbroken expanse of green vegetation interspersed with lakes and streams.

Thirty minutes into the run, he had crossed the 50th parallel and noticed a distinctly colder temperature. He was beginning to get an uneasy feeling as he passed through a few thick fog banks with zero visibility. The dispatch at Lac St. Jean did not mention any such weather. Weather in the northern latitudes was very unpredictable. He called for a weather update and was informed that a fog bank had reached the village. That information got his attention!

He maintained his current course, speed, and altitude until he received a signal directly from the village. He was out twenty miles from the village when a call came from a man with an Irish accent. "This is native Village Patok calling *Golden Angel*, do you read me?"

"I read you loud and clear, Patok. I'm at an elevation of four hundred feet and following your signal."

"We have a heavy fog bank that has enveloped the village and parts of the lake. Do you have landing lights to assist in making a landing?"

"*Golden Angel* to Patok, affirmative."

"Good, maintain course and when you're directly above me, I'll instruct you to begin flying in a circle of about a half mile radius south of the signal and slowly decrease your elevation maintaining that circle. We have ignited a large bonfire that you should be able to see. Tell me when you can see it."

Alvin was concerned. He was putting his plane and his life in the hands of a total stranger and was wondering if he had made a mistake in taking this flight.

"*Golden Angel,* begin a turn to the south and look to your right for the bonfire. Do you see it?"

He dropped two hundred feet, maintaining the tight circle when he saw the bonfire. At last, a specific point of reference!

"This is Patok. Center your plane directly over the bonfire and turn on every light you have on the craft. You should be able to see the water now."

Slightly above the water there was a thin layer of fog-free air. "I see it, and I'm going in for a landing. I'll idle to the beach for loading of the patient. Have the patient ready for transport."

Alvin turned the plane towards land and the bonfire. He killed the engine and stepped out into the water which was red with blood from dead seals and whales. A heavy-set man with a beard made his way to the plane. "I'm Father O'Henry, the Catholic priest for the village. I'm the one who talked to you on the radio."

"I'm glad to meet you, Father," Alvin shook his hand. "There's room for the patient in the rear compartment of the plane."

Several men were carrying the stretcher to the water's edge. "Do any of you speak English?" Alvin asked.

"Most speak some English, Mr. Starr. The injured man's name is Ocala. He fell off a cliff and has badly injured his legs and back. Our infirmary nurse has bound him for the voyage to an outside hospital, sedating him so that he will remain quiet during the flight."

"I'm anxious to get underway, Father. I'll help the men position Ocala so that he'll be comfortable on the plane's floor. Within less than two hours we'll be at Lac St. Jean."

"Oh, no, Sir." The priest interrupted. "There is no hospital there capable to help Ocala. He must go to Quebec."

"Quebec will push me to the limit of my gasoline, Father. Do you by chance have any aviation fuel in the village?"

"Yes, we do, Mr. Starr," Father O'Henry exclaimed, directing the men to the shed-like building close to the water's edge. They quickly came out with six five-gallon cans in wheelbarrows to the water's edge.

"Thirty gallons will make the difference, Father," Alvin cheerfully said, beginning to pour the cans of fuel into the plane's tank. "I'm anxious to be underway. We'll have Ocala in Quebec in less than three hours." He shook hands with the husky priest and started the engine. Even with the landing lights on full, he could hardly make out the water. He was concerned that there might be some log or flotsam to damage his floats. It was a gamble. He applied full power to pull away from the beach and became airborne without an incident, setting a course directly for Quebec City.

The higher he flew, the clearer the sky became. He checked his watch, it was one-thirty. He had plenty of time to get home by dark. He caught glimpses of the sun riding high above him. It was always reassuring to have clear skies in unfamiliar territory.

Two hundred miles from Quebec City he was alerted by a call: "*Golden Angel*, this is RCAF *Snowbird*. We are going to accompany you into Quebec City. We've been monitoring your flight to and from Lake Albanel. Welcome to Canada. We are on your port side."

He looked to his left and saw an RCAF fighter jet riding at his wingtip. He waved to the pilot, "This is *Golden Angel*. I'm honored to have such an escort. Do I have permission to land on the Saint Lawrence River in front of the Chateau Frontenac?"

"That area has already been cleared, *Golden Angel*. An ambulance crew will be standing by, and the Canadian Coast Guard is clearing your landing area of all boat traffic. We appreciate your offer of assistance. The local hospital is prepared to receive the young man. I'm proud to escort you to the city. The skies have also been cleared for your passage. Your call signal is appropriate and unique."

"Thanks, *Snowbird*, I'm a retired American Coast Guardsman and have spent countless hours working with your Canadian Coast Guard. It's nice to have neighbors helping neighbors."

"You said it well, *Golden Angel*."

As he approached the heavily populated Quebec he was instructed to follow *Snowbird* north of the city, then turn south to the Saint Lawrence River. "Roger, *Snowbird*. I see the Chateau Frontenac. The Canadian Coast Guard are marking my landing area. Thank you for the VIP treatment. I'm beginning my descent to the water."

"Good luck, *Golden Angel*. It's been a pleasure to accompany you."

Alvin saw the ambulance and a crew of men waiting for him on the massive dock area in front of the famous hotel. The Canadian Coast Guard had a small patrol boat close to dockside to assist him in securing the plane. He landed and idled to the dock where eager hands caught his rope and tied him to the pier. Two Canadian Coast Guardsman helped him pass the stretcher to the ambulance crew. One minute later, Ocala was on his way to competent medical attention.

He was relieved to have completed the mission. His immediate concern was fuel to complete his flight back to Greenville. "Can I get any aviation gasoline for my plane?" he asked the Canadian Coast Guardsman in charge of the patrol boat.

"Yes, Sir, we have aviation fuel on board the patrol boat and a transfer hose to fill your tank with fuel."

"That will be great, Ensign. I notice the Coast Guard Cutter NORTHLAND standing by across the Saint Lawrence. I served on it several times over the years."

"The ship's captain is Commander Lynch. He requested that I take good care of his former chief petty officer, and to convey a 'well done' from him and the crew. We add our congratulations too."

"Ensign, would you by any chance have a coffee station on your patrol boat?"

Ensign O'Hare smiled at him. "You know, Commander Lynch told me to be prepared to have coffee available for you. Yes, I've instructed the crew to make a fresh pot, and I'll be glad to join you, Chief. Our coffee station is a busy spot. My men will come alongside to refuel you. We're honored to welcome you aboard."

Two hours later, Alvin came in for a landing at Folsom's for fuel. He went to the closest restaurant to eat something and then checked the hospital to see if Lois's mother had been discharged. He saw her Rambler in the parking lot and entered the hospital. Lois saw him and ran down the corridor to embrace him. "I'm so glad you could make it, Alvin."

She looked into his eyes and said, "You look tired. Is anything wrong?"

He told her about the flight into northern Canada.

"Good Lord, no wonder you're exhausted. Have you eaten yet?"

"Yes, I just came from the restaurant."

"Mother is being discharged. I'm taking her home this evening. She's anxious to get out of the hospital."

He smiled. "I would expect that of her. I'll say 'hello' and be on my way. I am tired. The trip taxed my skills as a pilot. The north country has a certain fascination, but it demands a rugged constitution. Conditions at the village where I picked up the young man were depressing. Bare survival seems to be an accomplishment."

He went into the hospital room to wish Mona Vienio good luck. She was much improved and was ready to sleep in her own bed. He had always admired her spirit and good nature, traits she had passed on to Lois. He kissed Lois and walked past the Episcopal Church on his way to the waterfront. He noticed a bulletin announcing that Kimberly Lambert would address the congregation that Sunday morning and was open to a question and answer session. It was a part of an Alcoholic Anonymous meeting. He had no flights scheduled for that day and made up his mind to attend her lecture.

Early that next morning he had toast and coffee and dressed in one of his suits for church services. As a young boy he had attended church regularly with his parents and had continued the practice as much as possible when he was in the Coast Guard. He arrived early enough that he attended the regular service.

An hour later, he followed many of the regular communicants to the hall in the basement of the church where he looked all around to locate Kimberly, taking a seat at the rear of the hall. The minister opened the meeting with a prayer and a short introduction.

"Thank you all for coming to this meeting. This morning we're privileged to hear from a courageous lady who has experienced many lows in her life and has grown stronger when she found forgiveness and empowerment from God. Folks, I present Miss Kimberly Lambert."

Kimberly walked up to the podium and looked from side to side at the audience without saying a word. When she met Alvin's eyes, she smiled at him and opened her notes to begin.

"Thank you, Reverend and parish members, for inviting me to share some of my experiences with you. I speak to you as an alcoholic and a recovering drunk. I'm no longer a babbling, embarrassing drunk, but am, and will always be, an alcoholic as defined by that fine organization Alcoholics Anonymous.

"I found myself filled with self-pity and depression when I learned that my husband of several years had been cheating on me and wantonly degraded me whenever he felt like it. He did it in private and in public with many of our friends. My self-esteem was in the gutter. It was a failure I was unable to accept and looked for any escape that eased the pain. Alcohol became the cure for all of my ills.

"Then, my four-year-old daughter, Lee, was cruelly taken away from us when she was drowned in an accident at sea. Already weakened by my husband's relentless efforts to belittle me, I gave up being a part of the human race. Make no mistake, these choices were wholeheartedly made by me. No one else was to blame. After a long period of self-abuse and degradation, I realized that my destructive habits were going to put an end to my life. That thought process slowly and consistently confronted my blurred view of the small world around me.

"Many good people helped me along the way, but I can assure you that change, if it is to be meaningful, can only come from within. Encouragement helps, but it's not enough. Lectures from well-meaning friends were not enough. Eventually I reached out to beseech a God I had abandoned for many years. His love became the only source of comfort for my troubled soul."

She continued along that vein for an hour, taking questions from the crowd and answering them with honesty and clarity. She was inspiring and gave a positive message of hope to those who related to the troubled journey she had so painfully portrayed. She was the real thing, not a celebrity looking for kudos from a captive audience.

After the meeting, Alvin walked up to the podium to shake her hand and that of the minister. "What a coincidence that we should meet again," she remarked.

"I noticed the bulletin board and decided to attend. I live here in Greenville. You pleased the audience, Kimberly. You had a powerful story to tell, and did so with heart and compassion."

"Thank you. I drove up from Winter Harbor. Moosehead is a beautiful lake."

"Would you like to see more of it from the air? I'd be happy to take you up for a better view."

"Your invitation is accepted, Alvin."

Chapter Sixteen

"The town has a number of good restaurants. The one at Greenville Junction has a great view of the lake. May I buy you lunch, Kimberly?" he asked.

"Are you asking me for a date?" she asked impishly. "You and I have known each other for such a short time, yet our first encounter in the North Woods has been a source of comfort to me. I accept your offer for lunch."

"What do you have for an automobile, Kimberly? I've been a car enthusiast most of my life. My family preferred independents over the big three auto makers."

"My first new vehicle is in the church parking lot. It's a 1953 Kaiser Manhattan. It has a pretty blue interior."

"My Studebaker pickup truck is also in the parking lot. You'll find it a little choppier ride than your Kaiser."

They walked to the parking lot where Alvin held the door to his truck for her. "It's a cute truck, Alvin," she smiled.

"Do you have any plans for the day?"

"No, I was going to ride around the lake."

"After lunch we'll take a ride so that you can see it from the air."

"I'd enjoy that," she replied, removing her maroon beret. She was dressed in a dark green pant suit with a white blouse. Today she had a small amount of lipstick on to emphasize her lips. She was not beautiful or showy, but she projected confidence, determination, and an air of soft independence that made her most approachable. Her eyes reflected some of the pain she had endured. The inner peace she had found was instantly registered in her poise and confidence. She smiled more often.

They went to the restaurant at the Junction with a beautiful view of the lake. They sat at one of the large picture windows for lunch and saw several float planes like Alvin's take off and land. They both ordered fried clams and had custard pie for dessert. She was captivated by the view of the lake, and her eyes sparkled as she watched the planes.

Alvin had a chance to observe her for the first time. She was interested in everything around her. Being able to view her world without the limitations of alcohol and mental demons of her own creations was still a wonder for her, almost as if she was experiencing the small things in life for the first time like a small child. She was a pensive person by nature and had the creative ability to lock into her consciousness the sights, sounds, and events around her. That gift of discovery gave her a slight air of eccentricity with an almost child-like enthusiasm. She was a complex lady who had been threatened at the rim of a volcano and survived the calamity.

"The custard pie here is the best in town," Alvin told her.

"It is good. What a lovely setting for a restaurant," she replied. "I can't make up my mind which is more beautiful, the Maine waterways in the northern forest or the ocean on the coast. This environment evokes a sense of place and peace where the Atlantic covers a whole spectrum of human emotions, primarily a struggle between life and death. My image of Lee's death still troubles me."

He had never imagined the contrast between the two bodies of water, but the more he thought about it, she was correct. Placid lakes and pulsating oceans were a contrast. "Why do you live at the coast, Kimberly? If I'm out of line, I apologize."

She replied, "You don't need to apologize to me. I'm staying with Elaine and George. They've been so supportive of my efforts. My husband and I had a place in upper state New York. I sold it when my problems became too consuming. To be honest, I've been looking for a place of my own. It's time I made that step. That was one of the reasons I took this offer to come to Greenville. I've had several engagements with churches, granges and school in the state. I've met a lot of wonderful people who have been burdened as I was. I like to think that my message will give others hope to climb out of their dark places."

"Are you ready to go to Lily Bay for a plane ride over the lake?"

"That will be fun. I apologize for carrying on so," she smiled at him across the table. "Sometimes I talk too much, and at other times I'm accused of being too quiet. I'm ready to leave if you are. Thanks for lunch," she chuckled.

Alvin drove to the cabin and stopped. Kimberly was quiet, taking in the beauty of the location. He opened the truck door for her and escorted her to the plane tied up at the dock.

"This place has a peaceful energy," she remarked. "It's a wonderful setting. You must be very happy here, Alvin."

"How could anybody be unhappy in a place like this? I'm lucky to have found it when I was ready to purchase a home. I'll show you the interior when we get back."

They flew around the entire lake, taking several circles above the Kineo cliffs that rise straight up from the water. After circling around Squaw Mountain, he headed east past Moosehead Lake where he pointed out a trail visible in the unbroken forest. "That's the Appalachian Trail that runs from Georgia to Mount Katahdin, the first part of North America to be touched by the rising sun from the east. There's a cabin where the trail crosses the Little Wilson Stream that my father and several uncles built during the depression. The cabin still stands in the forest for hunting and fishing trips. I have many wonderful memories of that simple cabin."

"It's certainly isolated," she remarked.

"I'll show you where I was born and raised in Monson. It will only take a few minutes to fly over it. I sold the house last year."

He took a turn south of Lake Hebron and pointed to the family homestead, and then flew directly to Lily Bay where they secured the plane. He walked up the pathway to show her the cabin. She was impressed by the peace and solitude that permeated the area.

"Simple things like this cabin add to the richness of one's life. I envy you, Alvin." She went to the piano and looked at the music he had. "Do you play the piano?"

"I try," he grinned, taking a seat on the stool. "This was my mother's piano. I had it tuned after I moved it into the cabin."

"What type of songs do you like the best?"

"Many of the popular songs are nice, but I prefer country music and folk music, especially the Scotch-Irish. I've always liked ballads and ballad singers like Eddy Arnold and Hank

Snow. There was a train song by Hank Snow that was very popular with the servicemen in Korea – *I'M Moving On."*

He then played the medley and a popular song of the day, *Canadian Sunset.* Kimberly sat in one of the chairs in front of the fireplace listening to him. She turned to watch him as he played. He had memorized the songs and concentrated on interpreting them as he believed they should be played. He had a peaceful countenance that shut out everything around him except the music. She admired that kind of focus. When he had finished, she stood up to announce that she had to leave.

"Would you take me back to my car, Alvin? I've got an appointment in Newport tomorrow and reserved a room at the motel there. It's been a wonderful day, and I've enjoyed our date," she smiled at him.

"Of course, Kimberly. I didn't realize it was getting so late. You've had a busy day. Thanks for sharing it with me."

As they were leaving in his truck, she turned to take one last look at the plane and soberly remarked, "Lee would have liked being remembered like that."

"I like to think she knows and does approve."

She nodded her head. "Yes, you're right."

Alvin parked the truck beside her Kaiser. She had been quiet on the trip from Lily Bay. He opened the door of the truck for her as she stepped out to unlock her car door.

"You've been quiet since we left the cabin, Kimberly. Have I done something to make you uncomfortable?"

"Thank you for a lovely day. You've been a very gracious host and a caring friend, Alvin. I really appreciate your friendship. When I started my recovery, I knew that I had to become reacquainted with myself. It was not easy because I didn't like who I had become. You're the first stranger that has come into my life, and I'd hate to lose our friendship because you may hate the person that I became. It might not make much sense. I know that many people view me as a nerd or an eccentric, and I can accept that. Some people scorn who I am and what I am. I've been thinking that you might be one of them. What I really want is for people to accept me in spite of my idiosyncrasies."

"Aren't you kind of harsh on yourself, Kimberly? Your creative disposition allows you to sense things that other people don't see or feel."

"Thank you, Alvin," she said, embracing him.

"Drive carefully, Kimberly," he said, holding the door of the car open for her to enter the Kaiser.

He could see that she was emotionally distressed leaving the parking lot, and waved to her before she disappeared around the corner. On his way back to the cabin, he calmly reviewed the events of the day. He had seen a different Kimberly than he remembered in the North Woods. She was more in control and was able to laugh and joke. There was a depth to her psyche that made it possible to define her in several ways. Depending on her environment, she could be a different person. Gracious and kind, she was always a giver, not a taker. Her ability to be awed by simple things amazed him. He was glad to be her friend, and he suspected that she had the same feelings for him. They had shared a traumatic event that would normally bond any two people.

The summer was half gone, and he sat down one evening to evaluate his business. He had been able to pay off the cost of his plane and all of its expenses. The balance he had in his checkbook could carry him through the winter months if necessary. So far he was pleased with his new enterprise. There would be a few trips into the North Woods to deposit hunters at their hunting lodges during the November hunting season. After that, heavy snow blanketed northern Maine.

When Labor Day arrived, the tourists who had flooded to Maine began their great exodus southward. Greenville and other tourist towns in the state became once again the property of the local natives who viewed the tourists with a love/hate attitude.

Knowing how severe Maine winters can be, he was diligent in cutting firewood for the season ahead. He had carried a couple of cords of dry firewood from the family homestead when he sold it. It was not enough to last the heating season, so he began early felling, bucking, and stacking additional wood to dry. His father had frequently told him that wood that sizzles had less heat.

The cooler days of late August and early September triggered a melancholic feeling that made him reflective of where he was and what the future held for him. The death of summer had always had that kind of reaction. However, being able to work out-of-doors with a sweatshirt on felt good, and the absence of mosquitoes and black flies was welcome. Long, difficult days of winter in the Maine woods lay ahead to also challenge his flying skills and his acceptance of the life he had mapped out for himself.

The weekend before Labor Day had been a busy time exploring portions of the Allagash Wilderness Region with several parties of excited sightseers. He tried to keep Sundays free for himself. He needed that time to maintain the plane and to plan his week ahead. He knew that he was refusing rides that could be profitable, but he knew from experience that he personally needed the time for himself. His retirement from the Coast Guard was going better than expected.

It had been a while since he had seen Lois, and he wanted to see her that Sunday before she left for Wells. First thing in the morning, Lois and her mother traditionally attended church, so he waited until later in the day for a surprise visit. He noted that her Rambler was parked in the driveway as he pulled in behind it.

Lois had seen him in his truck and darted for the door, meeting him on the porch. "I was hoping you'd drop by, Alvin," she exclaimed, embracing him. "I'm all packed and ready to leave for Wells first thing in the morning. I tried to call you earlier and got no answer. I had a feeling you'd stop by."

"I've felt guilty not seeing more of you, Lois. Time has flown by this summer. I don't complain, except that flying has kept me from seeing my friends more often. May I take you out to lunch?"

"Mother has planned a boiled dinner. Why don't you share it with us?" she asked, leading him into the kitchen where Mrs. Carson was lifting a heavy pot from the stove.

"You're just in time, Alvin. Lois has been hoping to see you before she left." Mrs. Carson pointed to a vacant seat at the head of the table. "Please take a seat, and I'll serve you. If I remember correctly, you liked a good boiled dinner of fresh stuff from the garden like your mother used to make."

"I haven't had fresh vegetables for ages, Mrs. Carson. Thanks for the invitation. It'll be a treat," he replied, taking a seat opposite Lois.

He was afraid he was overeating the delicious boiled dinner, but Mrs. Carson beamed that he was enjoying her cooking. "You have a healthy appetite, Alvin. It's nice to feed a hungry man again."

They relaxed over coffee and boulla rolls, talking about those happy moments they shared as children growing up in a small town in rural Maine prior to the Second World War. It was a nostalgic interlude that left the three of them in a reflective mood. That innocent period in their lives was cherished by both Lois and Alvin.

"You know, I haven't been out to the Little Wilson Falls since we were kids. How about it, Lois, what do you say if we take a ride out there?" Alvin exclaimed excitedly. "It was always a peaceful place unspoiled by heavy tourist traffic. Probably because it's a little off the beaten path."

"I'd love that, Alvin," Lois replied with a smile. "I'll help Mom clear the table."

Mrs. Carson rose from the table and insisted that they leave to enjoy the afternoon. "You two run along now! Too many people in the kitchen are a nuisance rather than a help. It was nice to have you, Alvin."

"Thanks for having me, Mrs. Carson. Eating in your kitchen was like old times."

They drove through Elliotsville to the place where the Little Wilson Falls was readily accessible since the State of Maine had established it as a scenic park. They left the truck in the parking area and walked to the picnic tables erected close to the falls. It was a peaceful place to spend some quiet time listening to the bubbling of the stream.

Lois took a seat opposite Alvin. He listened to the song of the waterfall and turned to tell her, "You know, I'll miss you when you leave for Wells."

She studied him for several seconds before answering him. She had always wondered if he was still in love with his dead wife even though she treated him harshly. "Are you sure you're over Meredith?"

"That's a strange question after all the years," he quickly replied.

"It has crossed my mind, Alvin."

"Well, I can tell you without hesitation that her unfaithfulness made me hate her with every fiber in my body. When she passed away, I found it easier to forgive her, but rest assured, I haven't yearned for her in years."

"I didn't mean to plow old ground, Alvin. It's just that my leaving for a new job several miles from home has made me think a lot about tomorrow. I'm not getting any younger, and there are times when I'm with you that I feel as if you were somewhere else. Am I imagining things?" she asked, hesitantly.

"This conversation is getting heavy, Lois," he brusquely answered.

"I know it is," she admitted in a conciliatory tone. "I apologize for being so inquisitive. What I'm really trying to say, Alvin, is there a future for you and me together?" She turned away from his penetrating eyes and stared at the falling water, shocked that she had been so direct.

Alvin had a premonition that that question had been in the back of her mind for some time. How could he answer it without hurting her and possibly damage their unique relationship of forty years? "I've been so wrapped up in my own affairs lately that I really haven't thought about the future. You know how I feel about you, Lois. I'll miss you, too, when you leave. I can't give you that specific answer you're looking for..."

"Could the answer possibly be the twins' grandmother at the university?" she asked, knowing full well that it was placing him in a position not unlike he was on trial.

"You have no right to assume that, Lois. Merci Lane is engaged to another professor at the school."

"I withdraw the question, Alvin, and I apologize for bringing up the subject in the first place. You must know that I love you and always have. I was hoping that you felt the same..."

"I knew my answer was going to hurt, Lois. I'm sorry I've disappointed you. Do I love you?" he asked himself out loud. "I don't know except that I trust you and enjoy your company and want your happiness. Do those things add up to love? I just don't know. I'm sorry if I've hurt you who doesn't deserve to be hurt. I'll miss you when you leave town. I really will."

Lois sighed and grasped his hands across the table. "I know that all of those things are true; I've always known. I'm simply having a hard time breaking away from home for the first time. I'm beginning to have second thoughts about taking the job in Wells, and that frightens me."

Alvin saw the disappointment in her eyes and felt that he had let her down. "I'll visit as often as I can, and I'll check in on your mother to make sure that everything is okay for her."

She stood up to leave. "My friend Alvin always does the right things. We should be getting back. I've still got some packing to complete."

Chapter Seventeen

One weekend after Lois left for Wells, Alvin drove to Bangor to see the twins and Merci. He had called ahead to make sure that they would be home. Merci answered the phone. "Hello?"

"Hi, Merci, this is Alvin. I'm free for the weekend now that the tourists have all gone home and was checking to see if it was okay if I stop by for a visit?"

"Alvin," she scolded him "you don't need an invitation. Anytime you have a chance, it's always nice to see a friend. I won't say anything to the twins. Your visit will be a nice surprise for them."

"Thanks, I'll see you early afternoon. I have an appointment in the morning with a specialist in Newport recommended by my Navy doctor for my leg. It's bothering me some lately."

"I hope it's nothing serious, Chief."

"I was lucky to survive the incident," he explained. "When they inserted the steel rod in my leg, they told me it might need attention sometime in the future. I've been so busy these past few months I've forgotten about it."

"You need to take better care of yourself, Chief. Good luck at the doctor's office."

"Thanks, Merci," he replied soberly, hanging up the phone.

The doctor in Newport directed Alvin into an examination room and asked him to remove his pants. He lay on his back and studied the doctor's facial expression as he examined the scars on his leg. He removed his glasses and asked: "Have you banged your leg lately, Chief?"

"Not that I recall, sir. Maybe a stick of wood bounced off the chopping block against my leg, but nothing else I can think of."

"The area where the bone has attached itself to the steel supporting rod is inflamed with an infection of some kind. I can treat it with compression bandages and antibiotics," the doctor said.

"I'm a pilot, Doctor. I need my legs to fly for a living, and I can't get back home unless I can shift my truck transmission," Alvin reminded him.

"You'll be able to drive and fly, Chief. I also see that you developed a boil under your kneecap that should be lanced to drain the pus. That is the source of most of your discomfort. Hold still while I open the boil."

"Go ahead, I've tolerated worse things. I'm glad that I listened to my instincts for this appointment with you."

The doctor drained the boil and covered the kneecap area with antiseptics and bandages, urging him to dress it with fresh bandages every day and to take all of the prescription he gave him for additional antibiotics.

"Thanks, Doctor. I've got a pleasant weekend planned," he replied, leaving the office.

He had the prescription filled at a Newport drug store and then drove north on 95 through Bangor to Alton. It was a beautiful day with a few large cumulous clouds floating in the blue sky. The fall was the most enjoyable part of the year in Maine, free of mosquitoes and black flies. The prospect of a long difficult winter ahead following the death of summer cultivated a melancholic feeling that always made this time of the year special to him.

He could not help thinking of Lois. She had left Monson with some reluctance, and he felt responsible that he was the cause of her discontent. He knew that she had always hoped for a deeper relationship ever since Carl's death in Normandy. Alvin had always liked her and looked upon her as a dear friend. He often wondered why it never went deeper than that for him. She had much to offer the right man who could win her heart...

When he turned into Merci's yard, Jodi saw him and ran toward the barn where Alvin parked the truck, jumping into Alvin's open arms. "You've grown since I last saw you, Jodi. I thought I would surprise you and Melody. How do you like school this year?"

124

"Melody and I have made a lot of new friends at school. She's in the house helping Grandmother make a salad for lunch. I've been piling two cords of dry firewood in the shed," Jodi exclaimed, pointing to the wood beside the shed.

Alvin smiled at him. The fact that the twins had accepted him into their lives pleased him. "Once the cold weather starts, you'll be amazed how the wood box always needs to be filled," laughed Alvin, watching Melody running toward him, her two pigtails tied with red ribbons flying behind her. He caught her and pulled the two of them into a tight embrace.

"Grandmother didn't tell us you were coming until you showed up in the driveway. Did Jodi tell you that our rabbit has gone from the cage?"

"No, I just arrived."

"Jodi released them," Melody explained.

Jodi looked down at the ground and said, "I forgot to lock the cage door after I fed the rabbit. Grandmother said he'll probably survive in the forest on his own."

"We all make mistakes, Jodi. Don't feel bad," he said, taking them both by the hand as they walked to the house where Merci was waiting for them on the porch.

Merci was dressed in an old pair of coveralls with her hair wrapped up in a red kerchief. "Welcome, Alvin. I hope you'll excuse my work outfit. I've been painting the walls of the living room."

"It's nice to see you again, Merci," he said, noting a spot of paint on her nose. "If I'd known that you were painting, I'd have come with work clothes. I do have a pair of coveralls in the truck if I can help."

"Thanks, but no, I've finished the room and was cleaning up when you drove into the yard. How about a cup of coffee and a blueberry muffin? The twins and I went blueberry picking in the woods this morning."

"I'd love a cup of coffee and a blueberry muffin, my favorite."

Merci told Alvin that the twins' mother had returned to Georgia, "We never settled anything, so I'm going to petition the courts to request custody for them. They need better security and a more wholesome environment than Celia has demonstrated." She served coffee and took a seat across the table from him.

"I think you've made a wise decision, Merci. If you need a statement from me, I'd be happy to do so," Alvin remarked, looking at Jodi. "I'll describe a good way to locate the North Star, Jodi. The Big Dipper can be found by taking a straight line from the two stars that make up the tip of the spoon and points directly to the North Star. It can only be seen in the hemisphere directly over the North Pole, and it is the only star in the galaxy that does not move." He handed a sheet of paper with a diagram on it to Jodi.

"Thank you, Uncle Al," Jodi replied. "I tried to find it the other night, but it was too cloudy."

Melody had left the room and returned with the violin in her hands. "I've been practicing every day, Uncle Al. Would you like to hear some new songs?"

"That would be nice, Melody," he replied, placing his coffee cup on the table.

Melody carefully took the bow and violin from the case and immediately began to play a medley of popular songs including *Wedding Bells, Tennessee Waltz, Indian Love Call* and *Anytime*. She smiled at him and began to pick up the tempo with an old fashioned hoedown, *Turkey in the Straw*. Her smile made him feel ten feet tall.

Merci saw Alvin's reaction to her granddaughter and was thankful for his unwavering support for the twins. He was the source of the inspiration she demonstrated every day with her music lessons. Her due diligence was to please him. The way he reacted to her effort had helped the shy little girl to find solace and peace in music. His enthusiasm had worked miracles, drawing her from a withdrawn state to a much more outgoing and confident child. Merci had been worried for her and was prepared to take her to a psychologist at the university. Even Melody's teacher noticed a distinct improvement in her interaction with other children.

"You're improving every day, Melody," Alvin told her when she had carried the last note to a soft, fading conclusion. "I never knew that instrument could sound so good. You have a soft touch that gives meaning to the music. Not everyone has that gift. I certainly don't."

She placed the violin back in the case and turned to him. "Thank you, Uncle Al. I can't wait to come home from school every day to practice on the instrument."

They both noticed that she used the word 'home' for the first time. It brought tears to Merci's eyes, turning away from him so that he could not see them. "Why don't we have lunch in the barn? The sun is warm, and we don't have to put up with mosquitoes."

Alvin saw her turn away and understood. "That sounds great. It's a lovely day. Can I help with anything?"

"Would you volunteer to do hot dogs on the grill?" Merci asked, walking into the kitchen.

"I'll be glad to," he replied.

Later, he started the grill and soon they were all eating hot dogs and beans, a traditional Maine Saturday evening meal. Melody was anxious to tell Alvin about her new red bicycle. "Grandmother told me that it's important for me to spend time playing with other children."

"Her accomplishments on the violin are very important, but it should not isolate her from interaction with friends her own age," Merci added. "I thought it was a good way for her to have fun over and above her time spent practicing on the violin."

"I think your grandmother has made a wise decision for you, Melody. As soon as we finish eating and cleaning up, afterwards you can show me your new red bike."

Once the dishes were carried into the house, Melody took Alvin's hand and led him into the woodshed. "The bike has got a horn and a light for riding at night," Melody proudly told him. "I learned to ride it when Grandmother and Jodi took me up on the knoll behind the barn and had me ride the bicycle down the hill. Jodi helped to steady me on the seat and pushed me. I was scared and fell off at the bottom, but I was able to ride it down the hill. Grandmother then made me go down the hill alone. It was exciting, and I really like to ride with Jodi. Sometimes we ride to the gasoline station for a candy bar." Melody was pleased to show that she could ride with Jodi and their friends.

While they were in the barn, two of the neighbor's children rode into the yard to see if Jodi and Melody could come over to their house. Merci gave them permission provided they were home by dark.

Alvin explained that he might be gone when they returned home. "You two enjoy your afternoon with your friends. I'll visit with your grandmother for a while before leaving. I'll keep in touch. You two have become an important part of my life, and you're always in my thoughts and prayers. Seeing how well you're doing with your grandmother makes me happy." He kneeled to hug each of them and watched them ride out of the driveway with a contented look on his face.

Merci witnessed the exchange. "It was nice of you to stop by, Alvin. Little Melody has blossomed into an energetic and motivated child this summer. The music has worked a miracle with her. If I had not seen it with my own eyes, I would never have believed it."

"She has done well," he added. "Your home is a model of warmth and harmony, Merci. I'm sure their father looks down with favor on your accomplishments. You're the one who has worked the miracle. The twins are fortunate to have you. Their mother is missing the best years of her children's lives. From what I've experienced, I would not bet on much of a change from her. I hope I'm wrong, but..."

Merci turned to him and answered, "I expect you're right, Chief. Would you like a cup of coffee? These cooler days of September I find myself drinking and enjoying coffee more than usual."

"Well," he grinned, "I became addicted to the stuff on long, lonely patrols in the North Atlantic. I'd love a cup of your coffee, Merci."

He followed her from the barn screen porch into the house. He noticed that the kitchen shared a fireplace with the adjacent living room so that the fire could be enjoyed and maintained in both rooms. The knotty pine paneling in the kitchen gave it a warm and comfortable feeling that was restful.

"It's a nice room. When I was small, we used the kitchen more than any other room, especially in the wintertime," Alvin exclaimed.

"We've enjoyed it, too. I grew up in this old house. Have a seat at the table while I put on a fresh pot of coffee. I think I need a little sugar this afternoon. My diabetes requires due diligence. How about a piece of fresh apple pie?"

"A country boy with a sweet tooth never says no to apple pie," Alvin smiled at her. "You've been busy in the kitchen. How many apple trees do you have on the farm?"

"About fifty, mostly Mackintosh with a few Baldwin and Saint Lawrence varieties," she replied. "How have things been for you this summer? Your flying business seems to have been successful."

"I love to fly, Merci. It's hard to describe the feeling I have when I become airborne. The act of defying the laws of gravity are invigorating. Every pilot I know feels the same kind of euphoria. I've been fortunate. The winter months will be slower and give me time to do required maintenance on the plane. Lois, a long time friend I grew up with, has moved to Wells to teach school for the year."

"I've heard you mention her. She seems like a nice person. Are you two serious?" Merci added hesitantly. "If the question is out of line, I apologize."

Surprised at the question, Alvin was asking himself ever since Lois informed him of her decision to go to Wells. "I'm not sure, Merci. We've been good friends since we could walk. I value her friendship, and I'll miss her... Since she left for Wells I've been thinking a lot. I've told her how I met you and the twins, and I informed her that you and Merle were engaged. I have a feeling that she views you and the twins as some kind of threat... I would never have brought this up, but you asked about relationships. I've been thinking a lot lately."

"The fall season is a time for reflection," Merci said, placing cups on the table. "I recently had a wonderful visit from a mutual friend, Kimberly Lambert. She stopped by to share with me that she agreed to a series of lectures and book signings down south in the Virginia area."

"I attended one of her lectures in Greenville last month. It was a moving experience for me," Alvin excitedly told her.

"She confided in me that the two of you have become good friends. That's nice for both of you. We can never have too many friends. I told her that you stop by occasionally for a visit. It was then that she left something for you with me."

"Something for me?"

"Yes, I have it in my study. No one knows that I have it. She asked my opinion, and I freely gave it. She was going away for several weeks and was anxious to share her work with you so she left it here. "I promised to give it to you the next time you came. Come into my study. I think you'll be surprised."

Merci led him into a room off the living room and motioned for him to sit at her desk. She then placed a large object covered with a white sheet on an easel in front of him. She had a serious look on her face as she lifted the white cloth off an oil painting of the face on the port side of his airplane. The painting was an exact copy of Golden Angel as the artist had portrayed it, with the name, Lee's blonde hair, and her beseeching hands. The difference was in her eyes. Merci softly told him that Kimberly had painted what she initially saw in her daughter's face the first time she saw your plane. Lee was forgiving him with her blue eyes and parted lips...!

Chapter Eighteen

Kimberly's painting evoked deep memories, transporting him back to that tragic time and place. She had portrayed Lee with a slight smile as if she was sending him a message of hope and forgiveness. There was no fear or grief in her eyes.

Merci saw the distress on his face and rushed to him, wrapping her arms around his head. "Forgive me, Alvin. Kimberly wanted the painting to convey her daughter's forgiveness to you so that you could forgive yourself. My dear friend, erase all of those ugly images from your mind. I'm sorry to have shocked you so badly."

He was upset and embarrassed that he had been thrown into such emotional turmoil with Merci as a witness. Smothered by her embrace, he looked into her eyes. She was clearly frightened for him. She had kissed him on the forehead. Feeling her warm lips he lifted his to her, and they kissed. It was a natural act for both of them.

She released him and immediately apologized. "I'm sorry, Chief. I was concerned for you. I did not think it would trigger such a reaction, or I would never have accepted the painting from Kimberly."

Alvin was concerned that he had stepped over the line of accepted behavior. "I'm sorry if I was too bold, Merci. When emotions run high, we often do things we would never dare attempt under more controlled conditions…"

Merci carefully covered the painting with the sheet and turned to him. "I'm sorry that the painting struck such a raw nerve. As for the embrace and caress, I do not apologize for them. They were a natural response for two people who have become good friends and have earned each others' respect. To interpret the act as a commitment for either of us to the future may not be realistic…"

"What are you trying to say, Merci?"

She slowly took his two hands in hers. "I'm trying to say that there is a possibility that you and I could find happiness together, but it would come at too high a price. I'm engaged to Merle, and to break from our long relationship would destroy him. I can't be a party to that, Chief. You're an easy person to love. I'm sorry that I let things get out of control this afternoon. I certainly do not want to put any strain on the beautiful relationship we've cultivated and enjoyed. I need and value your friendship. True friends are even more rare than true lovers."

Alvin was dumbfounded and confused by her lengthy monologue. Was he prepared to commit himself to Merci now this afternoon? Is she the choice he wanted for the rest of his life? Or was it Lois, the faithful schoolmate? The questions ran through his mind like a restless river following the laws of gravity, flowing rapidly to the sea.

At that same time, Merci sat in a chair and stared into the ashes on the hearth of the fireplace. Her mind was working overtime with visions of what could be. What did she really want to do? Did she love Alvin, and if so, did she love him more than Merle? Did Alvin really come for a visit more for the twins or for her?

The room was filled with unspoken thoughts from two people who a few months ago were total strangers. Questions were rampant: answers were scarce or non-existent...

Alvin broke the silence, asking in a strained voice: "May I take another look at the painting, Merci?"

"Of course," she replied, thankful that the hurtful discord had been interrupted. "Maybe more light will give you a better chance to evaluate Kimberly's work." She placed the painting on the easel and turned a reading lamp shade so that it showered the oil painting with more light.

"Thanks, now that does help, Merci. The extra light highlights the difference from the one on my plane. They both have her blonde hair and blue eyes. My painting showed the fear and terror that I saw in little Lee's eyes that last moment she was above the water. Kimberly's interpretation expresses forgiveness and exonerates my failure to help her... I never forgave myself..."

132

Merci was quick to intercede upon his trauma. "I think Kimberly has given you a marvelous gift, Chief. If precious little Lee forgives you, and her mother forgives you, why can't you do the same for yourself?"

The question was simply presented. The reality quickly came to him, and the tension in the room subsided. "I think you're right, Merci."

"Kimberly's a thoughtful person who wanted to relieve a friend of torturing thoughts that can be too painful to maintain for any length of time," Merci mentioned with measured words. "I think she's a very generous person with a warm heart."

"Her virtues and unselfish character are traits that also define you, Merci."

"You're being kind, Chief"

"No," he replied firmly. "I'm being factual, Merci. Now, may I have the privilege of bringing this heavy conversation to a conclusion? I'm not sorry that I kissed you, and I enjoyed it very much. If you say it cannot be the genesis of a new and more meaningful relationship, I can accept that without a problem. I'm proud to call you my friend. I'll take the painting. Thanks for passing it on to me. 'Au revoir,' gentle lady."

She embraced him, looked into his eyes, and smiled. "Good friends traditionally embrace."

He returned her smile and held her in a bear hug. "Merle is one lucky man!"

He left Merci's house with much on his mind and drove slowly to Monson where he stopped to see how Lois's mother was getting along.   As soon as he turned into the driveway, he noticed Lois's Rambler and was glad to have a chance to see her. He walked quickly across the porch to knock on the door.

Mrs. Carson opened the door and exclaimed, "My, what a pleasant surprise, Alvin. We were just talking about you. Lois is in the kitchen with a new friend from Wells."

Alvin embraced her, noting that she had good color and looked better than the last time he saw her. He looked over her shoulder and saw Lois rushing into the vestibule. "I called you earlier, and you were not home. I was going to call you again, and here you show up at the door."

He released Mrs. Carson and opened his arms to Lois who lifted her lips to him. "I was pleased to see your Rambler."

"Come, Alvin. I want you to meet a friend from Wells."

She led him into the kitchen where he saw a man of medium build with a small mustache sitting at the familiar table drinking a cup of coffee. "Harvey, this is an old friend of many years, Alvin Starr. Alvin, meet Harvey Long, a school teacher at Wells High School."

"I'm glad to meet you, Harvey," Alvin responded, offering his hand to the teacher. "I stopped by to check on Mrs. Carson and was pleasantly surprised to see Lois's Rambler in the drive."

"I've heard a lot about you, Alvin. Lois has told me that you started a flying service at Moosehead. I flew P-38's in the Pacific war."

"Do you still fly, Harvey?"

"I haven't for a long time. College took up all of my time after the war. I still miss the thrill of lifting off the ground. Those who do fly know what I mean," Harvey smiled at Alvin.

Alvin knew exactly what Harvey meant. It was a universal experience among fliers of every type.

"Please sit down and have a cup of coffee, Alvin," Mrs. Carson pointed to a chair beside her and across from Lois.

"Do you by any chance have any boulla rolls?" he sheepishly asked.

"Only a fresh batch that's still warm," Mrs. Carson replied, placing a tray of rolls in front of him.

"Thanks, Mrs. Carson, they're my favorite treat," he exclaimed, turning to Lois. "Well, how do you like teaching at Wells, Lois?"

"Kids are kids, no matter where you go," she smiled at him. "I found the pace a little more demanding than here in Monson, but I'm glad I made the choice. I rented a cottage at the beach and find it relaxing and peaceful. The sea has its attractions as you well know."

Alvin and Lois had been raised inland from the ocean, and when he joined the Coast Guard he also found the ocean fascinating. "Lake Hebron and other freshwater bodies have that special comfortable aura that soothes the nerves. The ocean has a restless energy that always left me in awe of its many moods."

Lois turned to Harvey. "Alvin spent twenty-five years in the Coast Guard."

"I still miss the camaraderie that exists in the services, but I'm enjoying my retirement. I wanted to check on you, Mrs. Carson, to be sure you have enough firewood for the season. I have more than I can use and would be glad to bring down some for you. I can haul a half cord at a time in my truck."

"I'll be okay for the winter, Alvin. Thanks just the same. I have five cords in the shed, and the new kerosene stove in the parlor seems to be helping a lot," Mrs. Carson replied, pouring his coffee.

"The foliage north of Portland is at its peak color," Lois announced. "I thought it would be a good time to drive to Monson to get some of the things I neglected to bring with me. It's a four hour trip, and I want to get back before dark."

"It's nice to see you again, Lois," Alvin said, finishing his coffee, standing up from the table. "I'll be in touch, Mrs. Carson. Promise to call me if you need anything. Thanks for the delicious boulla rolls. It's been nice meeting you, Harvey."

Lois walked him to the front door on the porch. "Thanks for thinking about Mother, Alvin. I hope to get back as often as I can, but you know how the roads can be in the wintertime. You look a little troubled. Are you upset that I came home with a new acquaintance?"

She had sensed his uneasiness. "It has been a difficult day, Lois. My leg got infected, and I had a doctor in Newport look at it. It's feeling better now." He did not want to get into what took place at Merci's home.

"Is Harvey's presence bothering you?"

"What am I supposed to think, Lois? It's a little out of character for you to bring a stranger on a four hour trip to visit with your mother. To be blunt, yes, but you're a big girl now and can associate with anyone you desire. If I thought you were developing a relationship so soon, sure I'm concerned. If he's just a fellow teacher, and it's your way of being a friend, then I have no reason to think differently."

"You're a very understanding person, Alvin. Harvey is simply an acquaintance I have to work with. Don't read anything else into it, promise?"

"Sure, if that's the way it is," he replied, kissing her. "Have a safe trip back to Wells. I'll keep an eye on your mother, so don't worry about her. I've already told the neighbor to get in touch with me if she's ill or in need of something. I love her for

135

her kindness and faithfulness. She was my mother's best friend."

"Thanks, Alvin," she said, releasing his embrace.

His head was spinning on his way back to Lily Bay. He recalled every word that had passed between him and Lois. He was still uncomfortable about Harvey's presence with his best friend. Had he lost her by being too independent or unappreciative? The last few times he and Lois had been together, she had told him that she loved him. He always knew that, and it warmed his heart, but she had left for Wells without any commitment from him... Why...? He searched his consciousness for an answer and came up with a blank.

Alvin had not checked his mailbox for the weekend and stopped to pick up the mail. A letter from Kimberly was at the top of the stack. He rushed to the cabin to open it. Alvin unlocked the door and carried the painting into the great room, placing it against the wall on the kitchen table. He took a long look at it and then opened the letter.

Dear Alvin,

A few words tonight to tell you that I will be away from Maine for a few weeks and had left a surprise painting for you with our mutual friend, Merci Lane. I'm not sure when you will have a chance to view it, but let me tell you why I did it.

Ever since I first saw Lee's likeness painted on your plane, I've entertained a remarkably healthy renewal of life that has inspired me to be worthy of her innocent love and affection. I wanted you to know that Lee does not hold you responsible for her premature death. To the contrary, she admires your efforts to save her. The forgiveness she is attempting to tell you in the painting is for you to forgive yourself and to be satisfied that you made every human effort to effect that end.

While I was doing the painting, I had the distinct feeling that she was with me and approved what I was trying to convey to you. A secondary message is that of hope for the future. Creating the painting was a rewarding experience for me. I was finally able to say good-bye to my precious baby girl. That has been a monumental achievement and has reinforced my desire to rejoin the human race.

Thank you, Alvin Starr. I pray that you'll receive some consolation and hope from my amateurish effort to convey a positive message through my painting. God bless you, Alvin.

I hope and pray that my efforts have not burdened you more. I'll call you when I know my full schedule.

Goodnight,

Dear friend...

Kimberly

Chapter Nineteen

That night Alvin tossed and turned in bed. His thoughts were filled with events of the day at Merci's and with Lois. His relationship with both parties had been warm and comfortable, but now, he was concerned that they would be different from now on. That potential bothered him. His busy summer schedule had dominated his time and energy to the point where he had probably taken the relationships for granted. Was he selfish to be upset that events beyond his control had placed a strain on future relations?

A third issue that contributed to his confused state of mind was the painting that Kimberly had given to him. He knew that she had intended it to be an instrument of hope so that he would be able to accept Lee's tragic death. He appreciated the kind thought, but the painting and the message Kimberly wished to convey had failed to change his mind. That aspect of the painting bothered him, because it implied that his interpretation was wrong. He was there with Lee and saw the terror in her eyes. It was too powerful an image to be argued against. Kimberly meant to be kind and helpful, and he appreciated that, but he could not erase an image that had been seared on his consciousness for a long, long time.

Early the next morning, the phone rang, waking him from a sound sleep that had graciously allowed him to lay aside those things he could not change. He answered the phone, "Hello."

A traumatic voice at the other end of the line spoke with a feverish high pitch, "Is this the residence of Alvin Starr?"

"Yes, I'm Alvin Starr. Who's calling?"

"This is Merle Stanchfield. I'm at the Bangor Regional Hospital with Merci. She's had a heart attack."

"My Lord. How serious is it, Merle?"

"We don't know for sure. She passed out at home, and I rushed her to the hospital emergency room. The twins are at the neighbor's house. That's why I'm calling on you."

"What can I do to help, Merle?" Alvin asked, checking his watch for the time. It was past four AM.

"I know it's sudden and a late hour, but could you please pick up the twins while we determine what's happening to Merci? The neighbors were very helpful, but I know that the twins will be better off with you in this emergency."

"Yes, I'll get the twins as soon as I can get to them. I knew that Merci had diabetes. Does she also have heart problems that you know of, Merle?"

"No, this came out of the blue. I'm thankful that I was with her when she had the attack. I had her at the emergency room within a half hour. Now you know as much as I do, Alvin. The doctor attending her has not spoken to me yet."

"Well, Merle, you did the right thing for her and the twins. I'll stop by the hospital on my way to pick up the twins. Maybe by then you'll have more information on her condition. Hang in there, Merle. These are times when we're tested to the limit."

"Thanks, Alvin. I feel better already. I'll try to have more information when you get here. Again, thanks for the offer to help."

"You're welcome, Merle."

Alvin hung up the phone and quickly dressed, grabbing a peanut butter and jelly sandwich to eat on the road. He knew from experience that these kinds of emergency moments required stamina and endurance, and a little nutrition was necessary to go through the motions.

An hour later, Alvin pulled into the hospital parking lot and rushed to a worried Merle sitting alone in a waiting room.

"Have you learned anything more about Merci's condition, Merle?"

"Yes, a doctor came out of the emergency room to tell me that Merci has had a heart attack, and that they have stabilized her. They said the attack was called a coronary thrombosis, and they have treated her with an anticoagulant drug. They are using an electrocardiogram to indicate if any damage was done to the heart. He told me it appears to be minimal. Blood pressure medications have also been administered. Merci's recovery depends on how well she responds to treatment in the next two weeks. If she responds well within that time frame, statistically she will be able to resume normal activities within the bounds of reasonable expectations."

"That's good news, Merle. How soon will she be able to have visitors?" Alvin asked.

"The doctor said she could see some visitors tomorrow, but cautioned me to not overdo it. I know she'll be concerned for the twins. The fact that they are with you will ease her mind. Stress of any kind is not good for her right now."

Alvin nodded in agreement, placing a hand on Merle's shoulder. "She needs you to lean on, Merle. I'm proud to be a friend, and you should know that it doesn't go any further than that. I'm not a threat to you, Merle. I never was."

"I know that now, Alvin. Thanks for being so candid. I hope to marry her just as soon as she'll have me. I've still got some growing up to do. Today has been a reality check for me. I need her more than she needs me."

"I'm glad to hear that, Merle. I'll pick up the kids now. By the way, I should stop at the house to pick up some things for the kids. Is the house locked?"

"Heavens no," Merle exclaimed. "I don't think the house has ever been locked up."

"Be strong, Merle. Call my number if you have any more information. If I'm not able to answer the phone, my answering service will take the message."

"Thanks, Alvin," Merle said, shaking his hand.

Alvin drove as fast as he could to Alton to get the twins. When he turned into the driveway of Merci's neighbors, Jodi came running out of the house, slamming the screen door behind him. Alvin leaped from the truck to pick Jodi up in his arms.

"Is Grandmother going to be all right, Uncle Al?" Jodi asked in a shaking voice.

"I stopped at the hospital on my way here, Jodi. Your grandmother is going to be fine. She'll have to stay in the hospital for a while to get well. In the meantime, I'm taking you and Melody home with me. What do you think about that?"

"Melody has been crying ever since Mr. Stanchfield took her to the hospital. She's inside the house."

Alvin placed Jodi on the ground and walked to the house to inform the neighbors about Merci's condition and to tell them that he was taking the twins to his place in Greenville. He then stopped at Merci's house for the twins to pick up an assortment of clothes and personal things for their stay of at least several days with him.

"Can I bring the violin, Uncle Al?" Melody asked. She was deeply troubled, having seen her grandmother fall to the floor unconscious.

"Of course you can, Melody," Alvin embraced her. "Bring anything that will help you to pass the time. We'll visit your grandmother in the hospital when we can. Do not worry about her. She's being cared for by good doctors and nurses. She would not want you or Jodi to worry about her condition. We'll pray for her to get well soon."

Melody listened to what he had said and asked, "You aren't going to be sick, are you, Uncle Al?"

"Not if I can help it, honey. We can put your two bicycles in the back of the truck if you want."

Alvin helped them to select several changes of clothes and under clothes. He also suggested that they bring some of the books their grandmother had purchased for their reading enjoyment. On the way out, he asked them to collect their toothbrushes and anything they may need from the bathroom.

On their way to Greenville, they stopped at the hospital to determine Merci's status. Merle was relieved to tell them that she was still in intensive care and would be for the next few days, and was pleased to tell them that she was responding to treatment, and they expected that she would recover and be back to normal. They were all thankful for that positive report. Merle promised to call their fourth grade teacher the next day to tell her what had happened and to possibly obtain materials for the twins to work on while they were absent from the classroom.

That night Alvin and the twins ate a hearty supper of salmon and rice and string beans. He surprised them with a whoopy pie and ice cream for dessert. He joked with them that the dessert was his favorite part of the meal. The phone rang just as Melody was wiping the kitchen table with warm soapy water.

Alvin answered, "Hello." He was surprised to hear Merci on the phone. "Hello, Alvin. I've been worried about the twins. Merle told me that you have them..."

"Yes, they're here with me. You can speak to them, but first I want you to know that it's nice to hear your voice. Merle gave us an update on your condition."

"He's been wonderful, Alvin. When he told me that you had the twins, I was relieved."

"They've been concerned for you and will sleep better tonight knowing that you're being well cared for. Don't worry about them. This is not a hardship for me, Merci. I'm privileged to have the twins accept me as completely as they have. I love them, too. You just concentrate on getting well. We'll be there when you can receive visitors."

"I want you to know that I've petitioned the court for full custody, and they've granted my request. I wanted to share that with you. Their affection for you is sincere. To be able to win the love of children is a blessing. Thank you, dear friend. Thank you for being a part of our lives."

Melody and Jodi spoke to Merci for several minutes. They were more relaxed and hopeful for the future after hearing her voice. Melody had been morbid and depressed to the point where Alvin was worried for her. Once she heard the comforting sound of her grandmother's voice, she smiled and looked up at Alvin as if to say, "Everything will be all right now!"

That night the three of them kneeled and prayed that their grandmother would be cured and returned to them as before. Melody especially was improved. Dreams of better days ahead filled their heads and hearts.

Alvin was up early the next morning and mixed up a batch of blueberry pancakes for breakfast. He ate and was enjoying a second cup of coffee while the twins were still sleeping. The phone rang and he answered, "Hello."

There was a long pause on the line and he asked again, "Hello, is anyone on the line?"

A high pitched voice replied: "Alvin this is Merle. I'm calling to tell you that Merci had another heart attack early in the morning. She died instantly..." Merle broke down and wept on the phone.

Stunned by the brutal message, Alvin became unsteady on his feet and sat in a chair at the kitchen table. He could not believe that the soft-spoken librarian had been taken from them. "My God, Merle. How can I possibly tell the twins? They were filled with wonderful expectations after talking with her last night... What does one say in situations like this, Merle? I know how difficult this call had to be for you. May God give us the strength to accept the unimaginable. Are you going to make funeral arrangements?"

Merle's voice was hoarse and wavering. "Yes, I know that she had made prior arrangements at the local funeral home. I'll be in touch, Alvin. Right now I'm not handling this tragedy very well..."

Alvin hung up the phone and stared out across the lake. He had trouble grasping the reality that, Merci, the soft-spoken librarian, was taken from their midst. She had the gift of reaching out to people. Her most endearing legacy was her unselfishness and compassion. He had been privileged to call her a friend, yet deep inside of his consciousness he knew that he loved her soft and gentle ways. He cradled his head in his arms on the table and wept. How he would miss her...

Melody was the first to wake up and come into the kitchen wearing her pajamas. She saw Alvin crying on the table and ran to him innocently asking, "What's wrong, Uncle Al?" She placed her arms around him.

Her voice pierced his sorrow, wrenching him to the sad responsibility he had in telling Melody and Jodi that their grandmother had been called to Heaven. He knew that the news was going to rip them apart and destroy their dreams for the future.

Merci had been their salvation from despair and sleepless nights, substituting order and love into their shattered lives. She had salvaged them from darkness and surrounded them with security, love and discipline. Now she was gone. He asked God to give him the strength and wisdom to shelter them from overpowering grief. How could he be completely honest with them without shattering their fragile lives? What did the future hold for them? Were they to be sent back to their mother, or worse yet, sent to an orphanage?

His inability to find the right words angered him. Merci's son, Robert, had been killed in Korea. That had been the first loss the twins had to live with. Then the irresponsible conduct of their mother had been replaced by their grandmother, whom both learned to love dearly. She had given them a new life in a secure and structured environment that allowed them to be children. Now, another part of their lives was taken away, leaving them more alone than ever. Alvin was more concerned for Melody than for Jodi. She was much more fragile.

"Why are you crying, Uncle Al?" Melody insisted in her small voice.

He sat her on his lap. She was frightened. He saw that hollow stare in her bright eyes, he had seen that same look on men in combat. He kissed her on the temple and gently wiped several strands of hair from her eyes.

"Dearest Melody. Your Uncle Al just received a phone call from Merle about your grandmother..."

"She's getting better in the hospital, isn't she?" she screamed holding onto him.

"You've got to be strong, honey. No, your grandmother is not going to get better. Merle told me that she has died and has gone to Heaven."

Melody's mouth opened but could not speak. A look of disbelief consumed her. Then, she softly began to cry with large tears rolling down her cheeks. She understood what death meant. "I never had a chance to tell her that I love her. When she fell on the floor all I could do was place a pillow under her head. She never opened her eyes..." A loud, mournful cry pierced her lips, and her little body shook spasmodically. Alvin helplessly held her close, calling upon God to help him in this hour of need.

Melody wrenched herself from his grasp and ran into Jodi's room screaming that their grandmother had died and wasn't ever coming back. It was a heart wrenching scene that followed. Jodi had been sleeping soundly and sat up in bed looking into Melody's sad eyes. He knew then that what she was screaming was true. For a long time the three of them clung together in silence, drawing strength from each other. It was a moment when grief shattered their innocent concept of life in the future without their beloved grandmother. Their world had erupted in tragedy, and all they had was Uncle Al. They turned to him for comfort and guidance. More than ever he became their tower of strength they needed to weather the storm that had been thrust upon them.

Alvin was aware of the role he had been playing for the twins, and he questioned if he was strong enough to handle the awesome task ahead. His first thought was about their mother who brought them into this world. Was she going to be an important factor in their growth to adulthood? He was frightened for the twins if she fought for that right.

Chapter Twenty

The two days before Merci's funeral were long and tiring for both Alvin and the twins. He tried everything he could think of to change their thoughts and to fill the empty hours of sadness. He took them up in the plane to show some of the sights around the lake, the cliffs at Kineo, and east to Mount Katadhin, the tallest mountain in Maine. That helped to fill the days, but it did not displace the sorrow and sense of loss consuming the twins. Melody was becoming more and more withdrawn, and that bothered Alvin. She was not interested in playing the violin with him on the piano.

On the second day, Lois called to tell him that she had Thanksgiving off and invited him to dinner at her mother's house. He then told her of Merci's death and the situation with the twins.

"Are you going to take them in, Alvin?" she asked, concerned with the sober tone of his voice.

"I already have, Lois. They don't have anyone else." He then told her about their mother and her inability to properly care for them. "The court had awarded their custody to Merci. I plan to petition them for the same thing. I've talked about the future with them. They both want to stay with me. I can't refuse them, Lois."

"I understand your situation, Alvin. Thank God they have you now. The poor souls... they've been through a lot at such a young and impressionable age. Is there anything I can do to help you, Alvin?"

"Thanks for the offer, Lois. I'm not in any position to make important decisions until after the funeral tomorrow in Bangor. What do you think of pulling them out of school and starting them here in Greenville?"

146

"If you were certain of having custody, that should work out for them. All of the schools are following similar teaching aids. If you found that the mother had a strong case capable of reversing Merci's decision then they'd have to be moved again. That would be difficult for them," she explained. "I'm afraid I'm not much help, Alvin. You and the twins will be in my prayers. You take care of yourself."

"Thanks, Lois. I'll be in touch," he said, hanging up the phone.

The day of the funeral Alvin helped the twins select appropriate clothes. Arrangements had been made by Merle, but Merci had prepaid and planned the funeral several years before. They met Merle in the church parking lot. He looked drained and weary.

Alvin embraced him. "Have you been able to contact the twins' mother, Merle?"

"I found one telephone number in Merci's papers. I called but the number was disconnected." Merle kneeled to hug the twins. "I'm sorry, Melody and Jodi. Your grandmother loved you two very much. What a sad time this is for all of us."

Suddenly Alvin saw Kimberly getting out of her Kaiser. She recognized the twins and ran towards them, warmly embracing them both at the same time.

"I heard about your grandmother's death from my sister and rushed to be here to say good-bye to a very dear friend who helped me more than I can ever tell. My heart goes out to you two. How fortunate that Uncle Al has taken you under his protective wing." She released the twins and turned to Alvin, embracing him.

He thought she looked tired and drawn with heavy lines around her mouth and eyes. "It's nice to see you again, Kimberly. I'm glad your sister informed you. Merci and I had a wonderful conversation over your painting. She was a good friend to all of us. We'll miss her. The twins especially lost the best friend they'll ever have."

"That is so true of dear Merci. Her kindness and generosity will long be remembered. Her ability to reach out to others was a virtue she had raised to a unique level." Kimberly looked at Melody and saw the blank stare and the pain she was carrying, and reached down to pick her up. "My dear Melody. At times like this, nothing really helps to take the pain away. Think of your grandmother as having gone to a place where she's at peace and where she has been reunited with her son, your father, and the two are rejoicing. They both know what you and Jodi are going through, and they would wipe away your tears if they could. Right now the two of you have two guardian angels who will always be with you. Even if you can't see them, their spirits are always close to you.

"No one loves you as much as your grandmother, and that love has not changed or gone away, it has simply taken a different form. It's still real and always will be."

Merle witnessed the scene with Kimberly and remarked, "Come, we should take our seats in the church. "

Slowly, Alvin took Melody from Kimberly and held Jodi's hand to walk into the church. Melody felt safe and secure in his arms and she whispered in his ear, "I miss her so much that it hurts, Uncle Al."

It was the first time she had acknowledged her grief, and Alvin was relieved. "It's only natural. It's only natural, Honey. I hurt too."

"You aren't going to die, are you, Uncle Al?"

The simple question brought tears to Alvin's eyes. "No, Melody, I'm not going to die. We'll have to help each other get through this sad time in our lives, but we'll make it because your grandmother would want us to not be sad all the time."

The church was a sorrowful ordeal, but it offered Alvin an opportunity to say farewell to Merci. The eternal question, "where do I go from here?" was the subject of serious deliberations in his mind during the service. He was satisfied that he had arrived at a decision where he was going to fight for custody of the twins. That decision made him less apprehensive about the future. With Merci as their guardian angel, he was more confident about the future and the welfare of Melody and Jodi.

Kimberly offered the use of her Kaiser for the trip to the cemetery so that they could all be together. Alvin thought it was a good idea. Her presence during the funeral and the burial made the ordeal easier for him. She was dressed in a black dress with a small hat tilted to one side over her left eye and a black lace veil that covered most of her face.

At the end of the funeral service, she had reached out and grasped his hand. "Is there anything I can do to help you,

Alvin? I rushed from Virginia to be here in time to say good-bye to Merci, and I wanted to see you again to explain the painting. I realize now that I may have been too hasty with it. Merci had liked it and seemed to be pleased to act as a go-between."

"Kimberly, I accepted the painting as a wonderful gift from a friend who has courageously taken control of her life. Your intentions were unselfish and gracious. I thank you for your kind thoughts."

"I'm relieved, Alvin. The painting had the potential to make your grief more difficult, and I didn't think of that until it was too late. Merci was pleased to learn that it had been a therapeutic exercise for me. She had that wonderful gift of making people feel good."

"Yes, she definitely was that way," he soberly replied. "I'll miss her a great deal."

Kimberly saw the sadness in his eyes. "Come, the funeral director wants us to get our vehicles in line."

The committal service was brief and well attended. The twins had been quiet at both services. Alvin hoped that they would be able to accept their grandmother's death easier if they experienced seeing her in the casket and watching the men bury it in the grave. As horrible as it was to experience, he knew that, in time, it would erase any doubts as to whether she was ever coming back to them. To cling to such hopes were self-destructive for a child or an adult.

Melody and Jodi had walked away from the grave holding Alvin's and Kimberly's hand on the way to the Kaiser. Once Melody had paused to take one last look at the gravesite and then looked up at Alvin and said: "Grandmother is now in Heaven with my daddy…"

The statement touched Alvin. It was then that he knew that she was going to handle the reality of Merci's death better than he had expected.

"That's correct, Melody. How lucky you and Jodi have been to enjoy your grandmother's love for as long as you have. Whenever you think about those memories, they'll warm your hearts. The ones we love who have gone on before us did not stop loving us. Your grandmother's love will always be a part of your legacy."

Kimberly drove them back to the church parking lot. "I'm staying with my sister at Winter Harbor for a short time, Alvin. If you need me for anything, call there." She hugged and kissed the twins as they climbed into the truck.

Alvin closed the truck door and turned to Kimberly. "Thanks for the helping hand, Kimberly. Right now my primary concern and effort is to see that the twins are well taken care of. I'm going for full custody of the twins the way Merci did."

"They're two lucky children to have you, Alvin. I'll pray for your success. It was nice to see you again. Will you promise to call on me if you need any help?"

"Yes, Kimberly. Thanks for the kind thoughts. We share a precious memory that has helped to make me a better person. Thanks for being a friend. Until next time, Kimberly."

She fell into his arms and kissed him. "Until next time, Alvin."

Chapter Twenty-One

Twelve Years Later June, 1972

Alvin was absorbed by the beautiful lines of the Coast Guard sailing ship the *USS EAGLE* tied up at the dock on the Thames River in New London, Connecticut. Alvin and Kimberly, his wife of eight years, had just witnessed the graduation of Jodi and Melody from the U. S. Coast Guard Academy, commissioned as brand new Ensigns. Four years ago, before graduation from Greenville High School, both of them were accepted by the Academy. Alvin's record of service had been an inspiration for them and was an important factor in their decision for a career. He had told them it would be exciting, demanding, and rewarding all at the same time.

After Merci's untimely death, which had been difficult for all of them, Alvin was able to successfully petition the court for custody of the twins. Their mother was unable to or chose not to answer inquiries to her in regards to Jodi and Melody. Over the years Alvin and Kimberly were unable to locate her. The move into Alvin's cabin was the beginning of a whole new way of life for all of them. He was a kind and caring father to them, and they grew in confidence and self-reliance under his tutelage. Laughter could frequently be heard in the cabin, and music often wafted through the hand-hewn logs with Alvin on the piano, Melody on her violin, and Jodi on a conventional flat-top guitar he learned to play.

Fond memories dominated his thoughts. As time passed, Kimberly became a frequent visitor to their home. One day stood out in Alvin's memory when Kimberly stopped at the cabin while the twins were in school. She had reached a crossroad in her life and wanted to talk candidly to him about Merci.

151

"What has Merci got to do with your problem?" Alvin casually asked.

"I'm the last person to violate a confidence of a dear friend like Merci, but you must know that she loved you, Alvin. She never said it in those words, but I knew her well enough to know what was in her heart. She probably would have married Merle because she had made that commitment to him, and she took promises seriously," Kimberly frankly told him.

Kimberly's statement was not a surprise to him. Deep inside, he had perceived that Merci had feelings for him. Their last encounter acknowledged that fact. It made her passing that much more difficult. Unfulfilled affairs of the heart could be hurtful, but hearing Kimberly confirm his expectations had eased the anxiety.

"Right now, my main concern has to be what is best for the twins, Kimberly. You probably realized that I had similar feelings for her. It was easy, of course."

"Yes," she replied cautiously. "My publisher has proposed to me and is demanding a definitive answer. My parents had always told me that one should always listen to the little voice inside of me. I've done that and can truthfully tell you that I can't marry a man I don't love."

"What are you trying to say, Kimberly?"

"I'm saying that I fell in love with you way up north in the Maine woods when I first saw Lee's picture on your plane. Every meeting with you since then has only reinforced those feelings. I understand that the twins have occupied your time and energy. That's only natural for a responsible parent like you, but..."

"That's true, Kimberly," Alvin had explained. "Yet something is missing in my life. Lois is still a good friend, but I believe she's in love with Harvey Long. Every time you've left me after a visit, I had the urge to chase after you and ask you to marry me. I love you, Kimberly. Jodi and Melody also love you."

She had come into his arms and thanked her God. The fulfillment of all her hopes and dreams was to be the wife of Alvin Starr.

It was a marriage blessed by all. Melody and Jodi had the privilege of growing to adulthood in a home filled with love and respect. They grew into the fine, responsible adults their grandmother had always wished for them.

Alvin turned to see Kimberly being escorted along the dock by Ensign Jodi Lane and Ensign Melody Lane. He smiled and thanked God for the blessing those three human beings had been to his life.

The End

Other Historical Romance Novels
BY
Clifton LaBree

A Song for Lisa A Historical Romance

This is the story of a young American woman captured by the Japanese in the Philippines, 1941. Like most prisoners, she was brutalized and sadistically treated with a cruel disregard for human life. Three years later, Lisa and her companions had reached the low point of starvation and abuse .....

Lake of Three Sorrows A Historical Romance

A warm spiritually uplifting story of courage, commitment, and sacrifice. This is the story of Dale Cooper, a battle-weary American soldier who served in two world wars.

Flickering Flame (Colonial Series Book One)

A historical novel, about the Cullen family who settled in Portsmouth, New Hampshire, and their participation in events prior to the French and Indian War. Freedom and opportunity were on the march, but it extracted a heavy price. Frontier settlers were ruthlessly killed and butchered by rampaging Indians lead by French officers and Jesuit priests who frequently incited them to greater levels of inhumanity...

Raising the Torch (Colonial Series Book Two)

A continuation of the saga from Flickering Flame, Colonial Series book one, of the Cullen family in Colonial Portsmouth. This is a moving story of love and sacrifice when a small colony had the audacity to fight for independence from their motherland...

Non-Fiction Books

By

Clifton LaBree

New Hampshire's General John Stark, Live Free or Die: Death Is Not the Greatest of Evils

Publisher - Fading Shadows Imprint

A fresh look at one of America's staunchest defenders of liberty and freedom. John Stark was a courageous New Hampshire citizen-soldier who fought in both, the French and Indian War, and the Revolutionary War. His pursuit of leadership excellence on the battlefield distinguished him as one of the most successful combat commanders of the war, and one of the least appreciated.

His selflessness, modest life style, and devotion to the cause of freedom are an inspiration that time has not diminished. He remains today the embodiment of the frugal, independent, and cantankerous New Hampshire Yankee.

Gentle Warrior, General Oliver Prince Smith, USMC

Published by - Kent State University Press. Kent, Ohio, 2001

The Story of one of the United States Marine Corps best General Officer. His flawless performance in Korea is a story that needed to be told.

About: FADING SHADOWS IMPRINT

Fading Shadows Imprint was established to bring to the public books of historical events and portraits of people enduring tragic circumstances of by-gone days. Hopefully, they will generate a deep appreciation and respect for the exceptionalness of the United States of America, and an appreciation for the sacrifice and selflessness of those who valiantly served for liberty and freedom.

The characters are fictional, but the historical events and dates have been seriously researched and are factually presented. Some books feature incidents during the French and Indian Wars as well as the War for Independence.

World Wars I and II are eras rich in stories that beg to be told. I've tried to pay tribute to the collective courage and heroism, often unheralded, that has defined Americans in every engagement. It was a time when the immortality of dreams and aspirations were defended by the blood of young men and women. There is a beautiful monument and cemetery in a small French village where thousands of white crosses and Stars-of-David are set in perfect alignment, honoring thousands of American soldiers who gave their last full measure. A large granite slab bearing mute witness to their sacrifice has the following words chiseled in stone: TIME WILL NOT DIM THE GLORY OF THEIR DEEDS. Another monument reads: VIRTUE AND COURAGE ARE THEIR OWN MONUMENT AND REWARD. Those simple words define the American soldier from the dark days of the Revolutionary War to the present. They are an American treasure, unique in the history of the world.

Every generation has its own signature and characteristics that uniquely define them. The World War II generation is defined by the immortality of the ideals and truth they gallantly defended.

The United States has freely given precious blood and treasure to defend the rights of man to be free, and we have never asked for anything in return. No other nation on the planet has sacrificed so much for the noble virtues of liberty and freedom. We hope that the selections offered by Fading Shadows Imprint will touch your hearts and generate a deeper appreciation and love for our country.